MW01182282

TRIALS OF THREE

What Lies in the Dark
What Lurks in the Forest

What
LURKS
in the
FOREST

To Bailey,
Enjoy reading,
— Bethany Faith

Bethany Faith

CHAPTERS

	Acknowledgments	*vii*
1.	The Dark Times	1
2.	A Suicidal Mission	11
3.	Return the Favor	21
4.	Discovering the Missing	31
5.	In A Moment	41
6.	Invisibility	47
7.	A Change in Form	53
8.	Forgotten	63
9.	A Lurking Enemy	69
10.	A Kind of Freedom	75
11.	Life and Death	83
12.	The Wrong Information	89
13.	Returning from Death	95
14.	A Haunting Past	103
15.	A Stained Sword	109
16.	Shattered Heart Pieces	117
17.	New Challenges Await	127

ACKNOWLEDGMENTS

Zoe M. Scrivener & Stephanie Hodgson: Thanks for helping me edit and revise this book. They were both kind enough to read my book and help smooth out the edges a bit. Without them, revising my books would be impossible. I greatly appreciate their assistance.

R.S.Sharkey: A big thanks to R.S.Sharkey for formatting the interior of this book and making the cover. She's been so wonderfully helpful when it comes to the technical side of publishing, something which isn't exactly my strong point.

My Parents: They support me and let me strive to do crazy things - like work on publishing a five-book series. I wouldn't be where I am without their loving encouragement. So a special thanks to, Mommy and Daddy.

God: Obviously, my strong faith in God is one of the main reasons why I write. He inspires everything that I scribble onto my pages, and my greatest wish is to honor Him through every story I invent. There are no words to describe the thankfulness I have for Him.

CHAPTER ONE

THE DARK TIMES

The wind screamed as it brushed through the leaves of the forest trees. Small, orange leaves fluttered to the ground in response to the strain of the air. No light shone through the forest canopy but the small, glittering rays of the moon that stretched to reach the forest ground. The rays of light danced in the air when gusts of wind came to shake their openings into the dark forest. It was a beautiful and terrifying night.

A girl and three boys trampled through the darkness, ignoring the eerie noises and fading light. They were returning from their long journey beyond on the mountains. Tired from their travel back from Shamayim, they hoped to return to their home town, Realta, on this, a very dark night.

David paused as he saw the light of a few fires in the distance. He could faintly make out the shadows of tents and a few figures. "Seems that we have reached Realta." he stated as the other three stopped behind him. "Through that opening in the trees." he motioned to the lights.

Emuna smiled and walked up to the opening. She peered

through to see the town. Brian followed close behind her and took a small peek through the opening and Gavin stayed next to David, leaning lazily on a tree.

Emuna was the first to understand what she was seeing and her eyes widened with horror. She gasped and tried to hold herself back from running into the village.

The once strong town of Realta had been overtaken. The streets were now lined with broken vases and bloody swords. The howling of the wind was now accompanied by the occasional cry of a child. The lights David had seen were no more than the remaining embers of fires that once were. All of the tents had holes and burn marks and they now lay on the ground, trampled down.

Emuna caught sight of a figure stepping out of a nearby tent, she instinctively cringed into the shadows of the forest and watched with big eyes as the figure walked into the small amount of light the embers provided. Her breath caught in her throat as she recognized the strange figure.

The person wore a long, brown cloak that reached to the ground. A hood covered his face and he held a small dagger in his thin, white, bony hands.

Gavin sneezed.

The man turned towards the forest and paused.

Everything went still, except for Emuna, who sent Gavin a cold glare. Gavin smiled sheepishly at her.

When the man decided no one was there he turned around and disappeared behind another tent.

"Anikulum..." David said.

Emuna jumped, not having noticed or heard when David walked up beside her to take a closer look at the person. She looked at him, slightly startled. "Anikulum?" she repeated.

David nodded slowly and sighed, "Not much is known about them. The first appearance of their race was shortly after Pavix's betrayal. Usually, they live in the caves... they have been under the control of Terminus since his powers were awoken. Their leader is darkness and their tool is deceit. Not ones to challenge. They've been known to capture, torture, and kill those who wander into their caves..."

"What are they doing in Realta?" Brian asked.

"I am not certain, Master Brian, I would guess they raged war on the town." David looked down. "I'm sorry."

Emuna spoke up, her voice barely a whisper. "Our families...they are probably..."

David nodded solemnly.

"No." She said straightly, a strange defiant look in her eyes. "They can't be."

"Miss Emuna?" David questioned.

"They are not dead!" she screamed, the volume of her voice making the other three jump, "It's not true. Your information is incorrect-"

"Emuna." Brian tried to persuade her to calm down, "There's nothing we can do right now-"

"No!" she snapped at him, all of her emotions over flowing into boiling anger.

She turned back to the opening and made a quick dash to the tent she thought looked most like her brother's. Brian grabbed her and spun her around to face him. Emuna thrashed against him, but her fight was of little use, seeing as Brian had a strong grasp on her.

"Let me go! I have to see!" she cried, reaching for the village.

"Emuna, stop." Brian commanded, he grabbed her shoulders and made her stand still. He looked into her panicked eyes as he spoke. "We will attempt, with all our might, to find them. If they are still alive, we will get them back. I promise. All right?"

Emuna took in a breath and nodded. Tears began to streak down her face, catching the moonlight as they fell to the ground. She rested her head on Brian's shoulder and closed her eyes, trying to keep herself calm.

Gavin cleared his throat and David and Brian turned to look at him. "Not to interrupt...but...do you really think it's the safest idea to stay on the edge of the forest for too long? Assuming what David said is correct, it might be a little dangerous."

David nodded in agreement, "Correct, Sir Gavin. We should be going deeper into the forest. We can spend the day there and see what we can find out tomorrow. Perhaps some of the villagers have found refuge somewhere. If we find them, we may be able to learn what happened here."

The four travelers wandered through the forest. Morning had come, but the sun provided little light through the dark clouds that shrouded it. The wind had stopped for now and the only noises heard were the crackling of twigs under feet accompanied by the occasional ruffle of leaves as an unseen bird flew off into the sky.

They had been walking in silence for a few hours. Emuna hadn't spoken a word since they left the forest's edge. Brian kept a wary eye on her, never letting her out of arms reach.

"The caves!" Emuna suddenly blurted out, a small twinkle in her tired eyes.

The three boys paused and turned to her.

"What?" Gavin said from behind her.

She turned to look at him, "The caves." she repeated, slightly more calm now. "There are caves to the east of Realta that young children retreated to during the Great War. Soldiers know about them. If a war was raging that is where my brother would flee, he would take his family there. We have to-"

"Miss Emuna," David said slowly, "Are you positive of where the caves are? How deep are they? The Anikulum could have very well found them...they are, after all, cave dwellers."

"No!" Emuna scolded, but caught herself before going further. "They are well hidden; to those who do not know they are there it will appear as no more than an ivy-covered hill."

"She is right." Brian said, "The caves are about fifteen

miles, or a good few hours walk, east of Realta. They are well hidden and would be a place of refuge. Only the best soldiers would know about them. If anybody survived, though, that is where they would be."

"Very well." David sighed, "Then we shall go to the caves, but, please, proceed with caution. I am still not entirely certain they will be safe." he looked at Emuna, awaiting her promise.

Emuna smiled, "Of course."

David smiled back in approval, "All right, then lead on, Master Brian. Perhaps we will reach them before noon."

Brian nodded, turned around, and headed towards the caves. The others followed close behind him.

Emuna reached her hand out and gently brushed her fingers against the ivy curtain that covered the cave entrance. She stood still for a moment, listening for even the slightest sound depicting human life.

Nothing.

She closed her eyes and let out a long breath. Her hand dropped to her side.

Brian brushed beside her as she opened her eyes. He pushed the curtain aside and peered into the cave. After nodding to Emuna, he ducked into the cave, followed shortly by Emuna, David, and Gavin.

Brian looked around the cave. Pots and pans lay scattered on the ground and a small fire pit contained a few white ashes. An empty, silver cordial lay beside the fire, the top of it had been chipped.

Emuna rushed up to the cordial and gingerly picked it up. She took a small, white bottle out of her jacket. It had the same design as the one she held except for the slight color difference.

She opened her mouth to speak, "They were-"

Emuna's words were cut off by the sudden appearance of a woman. Her face slowly emerged into the light as she walked, timidly, to meet the four visitors.

She was an older woman - maybe in her late sixties - with a thin cloak wrapping around her long, green dress that reached to her ankles and puddled at her feet, her blonde hair reached to her knees. Her green eyes lit up as she looked from Emuna to Brian to Gavin and back to Emuna again. A smile of pure joy spread across her tired face.

"Emuna, Brian, and Gavin!" she shouted happily, "I never thought I would see you again!"

"Lady Maeve." Emuna said as she stood up. "Are you the only one here?" she asked.

Maeve's facial expression changed to that of sadness and she lowered her eyes in despair. "Yes, I'm afraid so. I tried to save the others, but..." her voice trailed off.

"What happened?" Brian cut-in.

Maeve looked back up, "Men wearing cloaks with white hands attacked the village. Some of us got out and hid in the forest, but, yesterday, they returned and took everybody. I was barely able to escape."

"Why didn't you hide in the caves before?" Emuna asked.

Maeve sighed and was about to answer when David cut her off.

"I hate to interrupt, but who is she?" he said.

Gavin spoke up this time. "She's one of the elders in Realta. One of the ones that used to tell us stories about the lands beyond the mountains and people like Lumenians."

"Ah..." David nodded, "Nice to meet you, ma'am. I am David of the Lumenians."

Maeve smiled and did a small curtsey, "Pleasure. I wish we could have the time for salutations, but I must speak with these three. I have not been entirely honest with you and I fear my lies have cost the lives of many."

"What do you mean?" Emuna asked.

"Follow me." Maeve said quickly before turning and vanishing into the darkness of the cave.

The group of four exchanged weary glances before hesitantly following the woman.

Maeve led the four of them deep into the cave for about an hour. Soon, they reached a doorway. She slipped under the arch and the other four followed suit.

They now stood in a large room. Shelves that held hundreds of scrolls lined the walls and a single desk stood in the middle room along with a throne-like chair. A pen, some ink, and an empty scroll sat on the desk with a few old scrolls that looked as if they had been around since time began.

Maeve carefully picked up the old scroll and looked at the small group for a second before beginning to explain.

"Every elder was assigned a scroll. For as long as we can remember we have been elders, instructed to study and teach the scrolls we were assigned. We would tell of the legends to the children, but in the secrecy of our small group, we would discuss the possibility of their true meanings. So we would search for truth of their existence. We came across this passage." her eyes scanned over the scroll as she read the passage aloud;

"There shall be a race long foretold of that shall fall into the lies of my enemy. Their hearts and minds will be deceived and turned from the very knowledge of my name. I will watch in pain as they flee from me and my people; hiding behind the mountains I built for them. I will watch as they destroy themselves one by one, through war and other means. Each of them growing weaker by the day while they think they have been growing stronger. All will perish; no one will remain. I give you this as a warning. Send someone beyond the mountains; to a land that is safer than you have been told. Send them. They shall save you."

Maeve paused and looked up. "I am sorry; I should have told you sooner. I did not know this time was now."

Brian, Gavin, and Emuna looked between each other; searching for the right words. Eventually Brian thought of something to say.

"But we just came from the uncharted territories and there was no talk as to whether or not we were sent by the villages...is there something we should have done?"

Maeve nodded, "There is another passage that says you are to defeat the evil and reveal the truth. Save those who are lost and end the dark times. We did not know what it meant, though."

"I think I might." David said. Everyone turned to look at him."Defeat the evil; Pavix is the evil. Reveal the truth; that of the uncharted territories. Save those who are lost; your town and the humans who have given up on the 'legends' as you call them. End the dark times; all these things will put an end to the darkness in the world we now know." David smiled, "It was written two hundred and fifty years ago, to lead the humans back to Elah after they had erased his very name from their histories."

Maeve looked at David quizzically, "Elah? Is he the 'I' in these scrolls, the author who wrote them? And how do you know these things?"

"Yes, he is." David said, "And, I'm afraid, that will be a long story. We will all explain later. For now, where do you suppose the Anikulum could be keeping those whom they captured?"

"What is an Anikulum?"

CHAPTER TWO

A SUICIDAL MISSION

The group peeked through a clump of bushes, gazing at the hut that held the last hope of their families.

Emuna felt her heart sink as she studied the poorly designed building.

The hut was about the size of one of the tents in Realta. It appeared to be built from stone and mud. Only one window accompanied the door and it had metal bars covering it to keep any prisoners from escaping through it, assuming someone was small enough to fit through. The dim lighting inside the hut made it hard to catch a glimpse of the interior. Chains hung from hooks on the wall and there appeared to be a person tied to them, but his face was impossible to see.

"I followed one of them here. I assume this is where they would be keeping anyone who is still alive." Maeve whispered.

Silence.

"Do you have a plan?" she asked to no one in particular, "You cannot merely go in and ask them to let everyone out...can you?"

"You are correct." David finally spoke, turning away from the small hut and looking at Maeve, "but we can sneak in and free everyone. If we encounter any trouble... there shouldn't be very much trouble, if we do our breaking in correctly."

Brian glanced at Emuna, who kept her eyes glued on the hut, silent emotions flooding through her eyes while she fiddled with leaves in her hands. He sighed and turned around to David and Maeve. "That would be a good plan, if we knew more about these Anikulum. Since they live in the caves, I doubt that waiting until nighttime will make much of a difference and, looking at the sky, it doesn't appear that the sun will be showing itself anytime soon. We are running out of options."

David nodded, "You are also correct, Master Brian." He paused and thought for a second. "A few hours or a day to think of a plan may help."

"Do you think we have that much time?" Gavin said, standing up. His own eyes were slightly glossy, but, beyond that, he showed no sign of his inner pain.

"Perhaps. We will have a better chance waiting and planning than running in now without a plan, or the faintest idea of their guard schedules." David said.

"Emuna?" Brian knelt down beside her.

Brian had stopped paying attention to the conversation as he grew more concerned about what may be going on in Emuna's mind. He gently touched her shoulder in an attempt to wake her from her daze. She kept her eyes straight ahead.

"Emuna, we need to go. We can figure out how to get them out if we just have time."

Small tears began to drift down Emuna's cheeks. She was hearing what Brian was saying, but she didn't like it. That much was clear.

"We will come back. We just can't get them right now." Brian whispered so only she could hear. "Even if I have to come and get them myself."

She nodded and slowly stood up, keeping close to Brian. After taking a deep breath and wiping a few tears off her cheeks she managed to speak up. "Do we have a better plan than 'a few hours possibly a day?'"

"We will think of one." David said, "We just need to get somewhere safer first...I think the chamber Lady Maeve showed us may be the best we can ask for."

The group stood in a circle in the large chamber. It was close to midnight and everybody was beginning to grow tired, but they refused the allure of sleep until a plan had started to be formed. They did not know how much time they had.

Emuna sat on the desk in the middle of the room, the end of her hair resting on the wood. She kicked her feet gently and watched intently. Brian leaned on the desk beside Emuna. Gavin sat on the large chair; he had moved it so it was a few feet in front of the desk. Maeve stood across from Gavin and David headed them, standing in front of the door.

"Why don't we raid them at night? They will not expect that." Gavin said as the group argued about the best time for their mission to take place.

Brian sighed in exasperation, "Gavin, we already explained that. Nighttime does not seem to be the wisest time because the Anikulum live in darkness. For all we know, the darkness of night would give them the upper hand."

"But, during the day, we would be spotted in an instant." David said, "And, if we assume they have Lupi on their side, it would be easier for them to track us. We would have a smaller chance to retreat in the event we are caught."

"So there is no ideal scenario." Emuna said, sitting up straight and jumping off the desk. "Does it matter?" she walked around the chamber slowly, running her hands over the scrolls. "With David, Brian, and my powers combined do you really think that we can't fend off an army of men wearing black cloaks?" she paused walking beside David. "I do not think timing matters. It is how we fight."

"Five..probably, really only four, against thousands?" Brian pointed out, "You know, I will be the first to agree with you, Emuna, but I think that might be too risky. The lower the risk, the higher chance of us getting your family back."

Emuna began to protest, "Bu-"

"Miss Emuna," David whispered, bending down slightly so he could look her in the eyes, "Everything matters right now. The timing, fighting, place, number of people, even how we breathe; nothing is too frivolous to think over before putting our plan into action."

Emuna sighed and relented, walking over to Brian and standing beside him. She twiddled with the locket that hung on her neck and continued watching the conversation silently. She would get her family back; she had to.

"Despite there being a possibility of it being our downfall," David started the conversation up again, "I think nighttime would be our best chance."

"Why?" Brian asked.

"We cannot be tracked if caught and we would have a better chance of getting away."

"At night?" Gavin said, "So...in a few hours?"

"No...I think we need to rest for tonight. We have been traveling for a week and it would be unwise to go into battle half-asleep and lacking our full minds." David responded.

"Agreed." Brian said.

Maeve had been silent up to this point and when she spoke everybody sat upright to look at her. "While I don't disagree that you all need to rest, I think we need to conduct our plan as soon as possible. We are unsure how much time we have, if any."

"The Anikulum's tendency to interrogate will buy some time. A day, at least." David said.

"Just because we have a day doesn't mean we should use it..." Emuna whispered under her breath.

"Sometimes, though, it is best, Miss Emuna." David

said, a finality in his voice that kept Emuna from arguing further, even if she did not, entirely, agree with his plan.

Brian's eyes shot open. He remained still, lying on the ground, despite the impulse to jump up and see who had made the noise that woke him. His mind raced to the last things he remembered.

After conversing in the chambers about an attack plan, he and his four other companions had settled down for the night. Emuna made a fire and cooked a few birds that David had caught. Everybody ate quickly, then went to sleep. Judging by the remnants of the fire, Brian guessed he must've been sleeping for at least three hours now; he would probably still be asleep if it had not been for the sound of someone walking that had awoken him.

When the sound of a twig cracking echoed in the cave again, Brian slowly reached for his sword. There was the faint gasp and the shuffle of feet as the intruder rushed out of the cave.

Brian thought he had caught a glimpse of the shadow of a girl. He forgot his military training and shot off the ground, not bothering to wake the others before running in the direction the shadow had taken off in, his worst fear beginning to whisper in his mind.

The woods seemed darker than he remembered. His feet caused twigs to snap and leaves to crinkle under them. The lack of light made it so Brian couldn't see more than a few feet in front of him; he was relying solely on Elah to keep him from running into something that could potentially kill him.

He ignored the scratches that he felt bleeding on his forehead. He had bumped into many vines and thorns in his frantic running. His mind was racing, intent on only one action. Stop her before it was too late.

Emuna reached the hut rather quickly. She paused at the edge of the forest to catch her breath. Her wrists wore small cuts from when she had pushed aside vines during her mad dash away from Brian. Typically, Emuna attempted to avoid going against those whom she trusted, but this one time was an exception.

I can't let him stop me. I have to save them. I can't go through this again...

She took in a deep breath and looked around.

The hut seemed lifeless, un-touched for decades, but she knew otherwise.

The forest was silent, and Emuna thought she must have lost Brian when she doubled back and hid behind a bush for a few minutes.

The distant sound of a nightingale floated to Emuna's ears. She remembered that song. The song she would listen to at night and hum in the morning. This little bird had been a comfort to her when she was younger, but now it was an annoyance; she wanted silence to conduct her plan and the noise was not helping her concentrate.

For the moment, she brushed off her agitation at the bird's song and continued surveying the perimeter.

Her eyes scanned the area. Other than the hut and a few torn-down tents, there were no buildings. She looked for another pair of eyes and was satisfied when she didn't see any. Everything was serene and calm. Emuna let out a slow breath in relief.

"This might be easier than I anticipated." She smiled and drew an arrow, paused, and stared at the item in her hand. She brushed her fingers over the red feather, pondering whether or not she would need it. Maybe not, but, then again, maybe...just maybe. Could she take the chance? With her power, perhaps, she didn't need weapons...perhaps, she could go in unarmed.

Brian felt his heart skip a beat when he saw the silhouetted hut against the small light of the moon. He let out a breath and slowed his running, Emuna was around here somewhere and he didn't want her to know that he was near. Silently, he began to search for her.

Emuna thought for a minute before putting the arrow back in her quiver. *I do not need it anymore.*

She closed her eyes and took in a deep breath. Every bone in her body told her to run in, to save her family, but the training she had gotten when she was a soldier told her to be smart, think twice; her heart could be deceiving.

The faint sound of a twig cracking in the distance caused Emuna to jump. She turned in the direction she thought the noise had come and stared intently into the forest.

She did not see anyone.

She let out her breath and continued breathing. Her hand slipped from the bow she had instinctively reached for and she slowly turned back to the hut. She studied the building, memorizing it and everything that surrounded it.

"Five minutes..." she told herself, "Maybe six. I have to do this quickly. Speed, you need speed." Her heart began to pound harder in her chest as she prepared herself for this possibly suicidal mission. This was her last chance. To turn away. To forget her family. She wouldn't take that chance.

"Emuna!" she heard Brian scream. Emuna turned around to look at him, but didn't get her protest out before he tackled her to the ground, shielding her with his body.

She hit the ground just in time to see a dark blue orb of a light-like substance shoot past where she had been standing and strike a nearby tree. It exploded upon impact and lit up the forest with light, the flash illuminating the figure of a man a few feet away. Terminus.

Brian quickly got to his feet and lifted Emuna up by her arms. He didn't give her time to think before grabbing her wrist and dashing into the forest. "Hurry!" he shouted at her.

Emuna ran along with Brian; half in a daze. Her plan had failed. She had failed. More so, she was being hunted by the only person in the world she could honestly say wanted her dead.

And it was all her fault.

CHAPTER THREE

RETURN THE FAVOR

Emuna began to breathe in quick gasps and her stomach hurt terribly. She felt as though they had been running for an hour, but she could still hear the footsteps of Terminus behind them. They didn't dare go back to the caves lest they put the others in danger, but this also meant they were to run and keep running until one of them passed out from exhaustion. Emuna felt she might be that person.

Brian glanced at her and realized she looked pale and tired. "Are you feeling all right?" he asked, gasping as he spoke.

Emuna shook her head tiredly, slowing her pace a little. She took in a deep breath and tried to steady her breathing, but only managed to slow herself down more.

Brian looked around desperately for a place to hide and saw a clump of bushes a few feet away. It wasn't the ideal hiding place and it gave little cover, but it was their last hope. He carefully coaxed Emuna to the bushes.

She gladly collapsed on the soft ground and closed her eyes. Brian sat down beside her and pulled her close in an attempt to hide them better, even though he knew his effort would prove useless in the end.

"I am sorry." Emuna whispered sadly after she had begun to catch her breath.

"It is fine...just try to be quiet right now. It will be all right." Brian responded quickly, straining to hear Terminus over the sound of his voice.

He faintly heard Terminus stop running and stand a few feet away.

Brian peeked through a small opening in the bushes, careful not to move too much.

Terminus stood in front of the bushes, scanning the forest carefully. His eyes ever watching, unwavering, and bone-chilling. A low chuckle resonated from his throat as he continued his careful search of the forest.

"You think you can hide?" he taunted, "I found you once, Emuna, I can find you again... Your friend cannot protect you anymore than your mother can. He is as good as dead."

Emuna's breath caught in her throat and she began to quiver. "Brian..." she whispered fearfully. Now that she was in danger and frightened she wanted him to protect her, she closed her eyes tiredly as she realized how ignorant she had been to run from Brian.

Brian placed his index finger to his lips to signal her silence. He shifted position and drew his sword half way.

"Come out and make things a little bit easier on both of us." Terminus growled, the anger in his voice growing stronger with every passing second. "Do not you ever learn? Running is useless."

Emuna opened her eyes and shuddered.

Brian nodded to Emuna and gave her a faint smile of encouragement before turning back to the direction Terminus stood.

Suddenly, Brian drew his entire sword and jumped out of the bushes, slicing at Terminus's neck. Terminus leaned back, barely avoiding Brian's sharp blade. He reached for the sword and grabbed it with a gloved hand. Brian twisted the sword, cutting into Terminus' hand. Terminus let out a small curse and let go of the sword before any further damage was done.

"It is that way, is it?" Terminus said sardonically as he dodged another swing from Brian. "Very well, little boy."

Brian began to swing at Terminus's arm when his sword grew covered by dark blue light. The light started at the tip of the sword and grew to the handle, slowly engulfing the entire weapon. Brian paused and watched silently as the sword began to disintegrate from the tip to the handle until nothing was left.

Emuna gasped and placed her hand over her mouth to keep from screaming in surprise.

"Well, that is positively wonderful." Brian said sarcastically as he dropped his now empty hand to his side. He barely dodged a large orb sent at his chest.

"You cannot say I did not warn you." Terminus taunted as he edged closer to Brian, slowly creating another orb above his hands.

Brian looked from the orb to Terminus, his mind rushing through the possibilities. "You know...I have something I want to show you." he blurted out as Terminus threw the orb at him. Brian ducked and watched as the orb hit another tree.

"Show away. Do not mind if I interrupt your presentation though." Terminus said as he began to create two orbs, one in each hand.

"Oh, feel free to. I do not mind." Brian responded, dodging the other orbs. "Just give me a second here."

"Ha!" Terminus scoffed, "No. Now or never." Terminus sent three more orbs at Brian, two aiming for his chest and one for his legs.

Brian didn't respond, but instead held his hands out towards the orbs. A stream of light came from his hands. He aimed carefully and hit all three orbs, disintegrating them before they reached him. Brian then held his hands apart, as if he were holding a box. His hands began to glow a bright white and soon a large, white orb was created between them.

Terminus scowled, "You too! Of course, it would make my life too easy to just have to kill one of you."

Brian threw his orb at Terminus, who quickly deflected it with one of his own and smirked at Brian.

"You are going to have to do better than that."

Brian glared at Terminus. "I am merely getting warmed up."

Brian held his hand out and a white sword appeared in it; it glowed with light and pulsed with power. The handle of the sword was Brian's hand itself. The light wrapped around his knuckle and protected his hand.

24

Brian swung his new sword at Terminus's stomach. Terminus's arm was covered with blue light and he used it to block Brian's sword. Before Brian could swing his sword at Terminus again, Terminus created a sword of his own in his right hand, thrusting at Brian's shoulder. Brian side-stepped and blocked Terminus's sword with his own, putting his full force against the sword, attempting to get Terminus's arm tired.

Terminus smiled faintly and pulled away, his sword disintegrating, "You call that power? It is child's play. I will show you power." Terminus held his hands apart in the same position Brian had earlier and waited.

Brian laughed, "I think you ran out of 'power'."

"You think wrong then."

Terminus clapped his hands together. The sound of his hands colliding with each other echoed through the forest and, in the blink of an eye, Terminus was nowhere to be seen. Brian paused and listened to the suddenly quiet forest.

Emuna's high-pitched scream broke the silence

Brian whirled around to see what had caused such a terrible call of pain. The sight he saw built a knot in his neck and he felt his stomach turn into a boat. Anger swelled inside of him and his natural instinct to protect Emuna fought against his training to think with his head. Everything collided with Brian at once and he stood speechless.

"Careful, or next time her cheek won't be the only thing I cut." Terminus said as he held a dagger up to Emuna's face.

She stood trembling in front of Terminus, his firm grasp keeping her in place along with the imminent threat the dagger posed. She had a gash across her cheek from where Terminus had cut her. A trail of blood ran from her cut to the small golden locket that hung on her neck. She looked at Brian with wide, teary, brown eyes and shivered fearfully.

Brian sent a cold glare at Terminus and took a step towards Emuna, sword still in hand.

"No, no, no." Terminus warned, pressing the sharp dagger against Emuna's bloody cheek. "Stay or the girl dies."

Brian complied and stepped back. The sword disappeared from his hand. He took a few, deep breaths to steady himself and waited for the next command. Emuna's life was in Terminus' hands now.

"Now, I think that we need to take a little walk. Talk about things that have been said here. Catch up, for old times' sake." Terminus said teasingly as he pushed Emuna forward.

She tripped and nearly fell, but Brian rushed towards her and caught her arm. He steadied her gently with his hand.

"Walk. Both of you." Terminus commanded, gesturing towards the direction in which they had been running from.

Brian nodded and led Emuna forward, though he could tell she was tired and ready to give up. Tears swelled in her eyes and she blinked them away quickly, doing her best to walk as fast as she could. Her only comfort was the gentle touch of Brian's hand on her shoulder. She hoped he wasn't mad at her, but how couldn't he be? She had brought them into this mess and she couldn't get them out. A tear overflowed from her eye and trickled down her cheek. She bit back a sob, but ignored the tears that began to fall from her eyes.

"Over there." Terminus growled.

The three of them now stood in a large opening in the forest. If Brian was correct, this is where the village of Yernen once stood, many years ago. It was now unrecognizable. The remnants of tents lay on the ground, trampled down and burned by enemies. The specific area Terminus commanded Emuna and Brian to go to was a dark corner a few feet away. An old wall made of stone stood there, poorly built and falling apart.

Brian hesitated and held Emuna back, "Why?"

Terminus glared at Brian, his fist clenched and his eyes flashed anger, "Because I want you over there." he stabbed his finger at the corner, "Go. Now. Question me no further."

Brian held Terminus' gaze for a second before walking over to the wall, bringing Emuna along with him. He stopped near the wall and stood beside her.

Emuna stared at the ground and played with her locket. She didn't blink or tremble, all her body permitted her to do was stare. Paralyzed with fear. Finally, she managed a small whisper and looked at Brian. "I'm scared..." she said quietly.

Brian sighed and brushed a strand of her beautiful, brown hair from her face. "I know." was all the comforting reply he could think of. He was having trouble covering up his own concerns and found helping Emuna to cope with hers to be a rather difficult task.

"No talking." Terminus said absentmindedly as he

strung an arrow, keeping it aimed at the ground for the time being. "If you two stand still this can go quickly."

Emuna's eyes widened and she subconsciously cowered into Brian's arms and buried her face in his chest, trembling uncontrollably as she held back tears.

Brian's face hardened and he glared at Terminus. "Are you entirely mad?" he scolded, "Do you have no heart? For the love of Elah, man, open your eyes! You would kill your own flesh and blood for power?"

Terminus scowled at Brian. "Do not speak to me like that!" He screamed.

"I think I will speak to you any way I please, seeing as you are going to kill us either way!" Brian said.

"Trust me, boy, there are worst things I can do to you." Terminus said, his voice lowering into a deathly growl.

"Oh, and I suppose you consider yourself noble for just killing us instead." Brian taunted.

"No!" Terminus said, his voice going back to screaming. "I consider myself merciful! You think I'm the only one that wants you two? Think again! I can name quite a few people that would pay high money to get their hands on you! They would do far worse than I'm about to do! Don't confuse me for one of them!"

"I assure you, I am not confused." Brian said. "I see a man about to kill his own daughter for his own selfish wants. The epitome of evil and it angers me to the core."

Terminus stood speechless for a second before stomping up to Brian and striking him with the butt of his bow, leaving a bruise on Brian's cheek. "I told you. Do not speak to me like that." Terminus said, his voice dangerously low.

Brian's face turned red with rage and he curled his hands into a tight fist. The only thing that kept him from attacking Terminus was the trembling Emuna that held onto him. Her eyes watching everything and her mind silently recording it. The day someone actually stood up for *her*. Possibly the first, last, and only.

"I will make it entirely clear to yo-" Terminus began, but never finished. His eyes locked on the gold necklace that Emuna wore, seeming to be hypnotized by it as the round locket swung like a pendulum when she moved. He fell silent and roughly grabbed the necklace off of Emuna

"No!" she screamed in protest as the gold chain broke, letting Terminus grab it from her and hold it in his hands. "Please!" she begged, "Please, give it back! I don't know what happens! It wi-"

She stopped talking and watched in shock as purple light began to surround the necklace that Terminus held in his hands. The light separated into two rings and swirled around each other, picking up speed until the necklace was not visible through the light surrounding it. They grew outward and encircled Terminus as well. Then they exploded in a flash of light causing Emuna and Brian to jump from the noise and brightness. When their eyes readjusted, Terminus was no longer there.

The gold necklace fell to the ground with a clink and shimmered in the moonlight.

Emuna shuddered and stared where Terminus had stood,

"H-he is...gone." she stated, lost for any other words.

Brian waved his hand over the air where Terminus had stood. When he didn't feel anything, he bent down and gently picked up the locket. "He is not here anymore, that is certain." he stood up and handed the locket to Emuna.

She took it gladly and held it to her neck, the broken chain preventing her from putting it on. "Do you think he is...he's...?" she took in a deep breath and closed her eyes. Whether or not he wanted her dead, he was her father and secretly, deep in her heart, she knew she still loved him like a father. If only he would have returned the favor.

CHAPTER FOUR

DISCOVERING THE MISSING

David opened his eyes, groggy from the long night's sleep on the stone floor. He sat up slowly and stretched his arms out, "I'm getting too old for this." he half-whispered, half-chuckled to himself as he tried to relax his stiff muscles.

As he stretched himself, his eyes instinctively scanned the cave. Gavin was sleeping beside him, as was normal. Maeve was also asleep a few feet in front of Gavin, just as he remembered. Suddenly, his eyes widened and he stood up quickly, rushing to the make-shift beds Brian and Emuna had gone to sleep on.

David forgot formality and called out to the other two. "Gavin! Maeve! Wake up!" he screamed as he dropped to his knees and searched through the old sheets that lay on the ground without their owners. He realized that both Brian's sword and Emuna's bow and quiver were not there. The realization of how much of a danger they could be in placed a knot in David's throat.

He had taken an oath the day Elah had told him to find the three teenagers and bring them safely to Shamayim. At the time, he had not fully understood the extent of his promise, but he did as soon as he saw Brian willingly give his life for his friends. He would protect them, to the death. For that very reason, the mere thought of the two in danger and without him sent panic through him.

Maeve sat up slowly, her old age making it difficult for her to wake up quickly. She took in a quick breath after noticing the two empty beds and David searching through them. "Where are they?" she asked, as Gavin stood up and grabbed his sword.

"I do not know." David said quickly, standing up and looking between Gavin and Maeve. "You two must stay here. I have to go find them or die trying. Do not leave the cave unless it is a necessity with your lives at risk. Is that clear?"

Maeve nodded.

"Yes, Sir." Gavin responded.

"Good." David placed a hand on Gavin's shoulder. "Protect Lady Maeve. I expect no acts of cowardice from you. I may not be back."

With that David turned and ran off into the forest, not staying around long enough for Gavin to reply.

Emuna stirred.

Brian shifted position slightly and consented to opening his eyes despite the pounding headache that threatened to erupt at the first sight of sunshine. He ignored the pain that greeted him along with the grey rays of light.

Emuna lay beside him on the leaf-covered, damp, forest

floor. Her hand held his gently and rested on the ground between them. She lay on her side, facing Brian, and her long, brown hair rested on the ground behind her. The only flaw on her face was the freshly made cut across her cheek. It was deep and it would leave a scar, but for now, at least, she was safe. The cut had stopped bleeding for the time being and was now only pink around the wound's edge.

Brian thought for a minute that she looked extremely peaceful and elegant. He paused to watch her sleep for a second, but quickly brushed his thoughts aside and set his mind on their current situation.

She isn't going to let me take her back to camp, not without a promise to get her family before the day is over. He thought to himself as he sat up slowly, his head scolding him with a dizzy spell and nearly dragging him back down to the ground. He shook his head in protest and forced himself to stay sitting up.

I do not entirely disagree with her...we do need to save those whom we can, especially our families. Brian paused and scowled as he thought of his family. *What am I thinking? I do not want to save my father! My mother, though.* He sighed and raised his hand to his head, rubbing his forehead. "This is a complex situation." He accidentally said out loud.

Emuna murmured something in her sleep and Brian turned towards her. She had taken her hand out of his, curled both of her hands into tight fists, and pulled her arms close to her body. She was obviously dreaming; Brian could imagine she was probably reliving the events of last night as he would no doubt do sometime soon, but not today. Today, tonight, and tomorrow. He needed his mind clear, at least for two days and a night. If he was going to plan a break in with a two man team against thousands of soldiers, he would need clarity.

Emuna let out a small yelp. She gasped and shot her eyes open, her body tensing as she awoke from her nightmare. Brian was the first thing she saw and he gave her a small amount of comfort, enough for her to relax. She let out a long breath and sat up slowly. Her body wanted her to stretch, but she knew it would only hurt so she resisted the urge for now and just looked at Brian.

Brian thought for a second, pondering the best course of action. He finally decided on one and broke the silence that had befallen the forest. "Did you sleep well?" he asked Emuna courteously, standing up and brushing a few leaves off his pants.

She nodded silently in response.

"That's good." Brian said, holding his hand out to help Emuna stand up.

She took it hesitantly and stood up, wondering what Brian was up to.

"Well, we should get going. Come on." Brian turned and began to walk in the direction toward the caves.

"Wait..." Emuna called from behind him, she had not moved from her spot on the ground.

Brian sighed, "That plan didn't work." he whispered under his breath as he turned around to face Emuna.

She glared at him with her arms crossed over her chest.

"I do not forget that easily."

"I know..." he said tiredly, "But I do not think it is safe for us to try to get your family back, just the two of us. Everything is against us, Emuna. Your locket broke and now you have to hold it in your hand."

Emuna looked down at the locket she held in her left hand, the only thing keeping her powers under control. She realized the chain was no longer broken and slipped it back on her neck. Brian didn't seem to notice.

"David is probably beside himself with worry about where we are now."

That thought hadn't occurred to her, she began to wonder what David would do to find them. Hopefully, nothing extremely dangerous.

"And there are only two of us. Two against thousands, Emuna. I believed in legends, what was said to be false, for a while, but I will not put my life on the line for something that has proven to be impossible."

"You fought against thousands and survived." Emuna said, half in a daze as her eyes sunk to the scar that ran from Brian's wrist to his elbow, encircling his forearm.

"I survived, but I was tortured for three days. Not to mention, it was a life or death circumstance. My death for your life."

Emuna sighed, "My family has been tortured for four days and I am not letting another day pass where I do not try, to my greatest abilities, to rescue them."

Brian carefully brushed his finger over the cut on her

cheek, "You do not think you have already done that? Please, Emuna."

She stepped away from his touch and quickly wiped a tear that had begun to creep down her cheek. "No. I did not get them back."

"But you risked your life trying, is not that what matters? We will have a greater chance of getting your family back if we work as a team. Trust me. Please."

She sighed, "I do not think I can. Everyone I care about is being tortured until death and you want me to wait for some sort of plan, that may or may not work, to get them back. While, for all we know, we could be out of time right now. I am going and I am going to get them back or die trying. You cannot stop me." she turned in the opposite direction and began to walk deeper into the forest and towards the hut Maeve had shown them.

Brian paused for a second then caught up to Emuna and settled on a pace beside her, "Then I am going with you."

Gavin told Maeve of everything that had happened in the past two months, his betrayal, Brian's sacrifice, Emuna's powers. But his favorite thing to describe was Elah. He went into detail of the sound of his voice and the meticulous way his tent was set up. Describing as little as the blades of grass in Shamayim and every line of dialogue spoken by Elah. He had obviously grown close to this kind man.

Maeve listened intently for hours, not even realizing that

time was ticking by. She grew thoroughly intrigued with Gavin's story and asked questions even Gavin could not answer. Mostly, she asked questions about David; where his family was, how old he was, why he decided to come to Realta with the three of them, even so much as his middle name. Something about this Lumenian intrigued Maeve, though she could not figure out what it was.

"So we came to the caves Emuna had remembered and that is where we found you." Gavin finished.

"That is an amazing tale, Gavin. Though something has occurred to me..."

"What?"

"Why is it that Emuna needs the necklace to control her powers while David and Brian do not?"

"That confused me at first too, but when I asked David, he said it was because her powers were awoken with dark forces. The necklace she put on when she originally used her powers contained forces that Pavix uses. The one she has right now contains Elah's power. Evidently, it protects her from...exploding or something. I am not entirely sure, but I do not really wish to find out."

"Exploding?"

Gavin shrugged, "I do not know. Maybe her powers will control her or she will go entirely mad like her father. Elah or David have not told us what happens."

"I do not think Emuna would go mad. She has always been a faithful and kind girl."

"Anything is possible."

"Emuna, you are acting entirely mad." Brian said wearily as he walked beside Emuna. He had attempted to convince to her to have at least a small plan thought out before she tried to save her family. 'I am going to go in, and I am going to get them back.' was the only response he got, which only raised his concern for her all the more.

Emuna paused for a second; thinking about the pain Brian's words caused her. She shook her head and continued walking quickly, ignoring the nagging sting that wanted to settle into her heart.

"Not mad." Brian sighed, now struggling to keep up with her. He was extremely tired today. Using his powers was known to fatigue him. Even David could only use his powers for so long before running out of his strength. And having to keep up with a very angry, very persistent, and very intent Emuna did not help with his tiredness.

His headache grew in pain and he grimaced at the pounding before continuing. "Just intent."

Emuna kept walking.

Brian grabbed her arm and forced her to a stop. "So intent that you are about to rush into an army of angry Ankulum. If you want your family back, Emuna, you have to use your head as well as your heart."

Emuna looked into Brian's eyes for a moment, lost for words. Somewhere inside her she knew he was right, sadly, but just because he was right didn't mean she would listen

38

to him. Angrily, she took her arm out of his grasp and glared at him. "Try to stop me then."

"I am *trying* to stop you, Emuna!" Brian persisted, "If you would just listen to me, please!"

"Why should I?" she snapped back, "I have not even known you for a year! To my knowledge, you could be attempting to trick me! I have no reason to listen to you!"

Brian paused, "When have I ever tried to trick you?" he said, "You know I would not hurt you."

Emuna glared at him for a moment, "It does not matter, you are trying to stop me. So fine, stay here, coward, I am going." she turned away and stomped off angrily.

Brian stared after her, speechless, hurt, and shocked. Where had that come from? Since he had met Emuna she had never been cruel to him and she had earned his trust because of that. Now, though, she was not acting like the Emuna he thought he knew and Brian felt his heart sink.

"Elah, help her." he whispered as Emuna disappeared into the forest, Brian no longer there to protect her from her own mistakes.

CHAPTER FIVE

IN A MOMENT

Emuna walked through the forest silently, a scowl on her face as she complained to herself. Her mind fogged with anger. She didn't even seem to notice the dark clouds in the sky that rumbled with the sound of rain threatening to fall down.

"How dare he think I cannot get my family back without a plan!" she said, "I am the strength of an entire army with my power! I will get them back!"

She took in a deep breath and let it out slowly, trying to calm herself. Deep inside she knew he was right, but she didn't want to believe it because if she believed it her last, small flicker of hope would vanish.

Perhaps he is right. She thought to herself. *Maybe...maybe I should think things through.*

She sighed and paused in her walk, deep in thought.

A slight ruffle of leaves from behind Emuna caused her to jump. She turned around quickly, her heart picking up speed. Instinctively, she strung an arrow and pulled it back as she scanned the forest.

For a moment, there was nothing, then a sharp pain in

Emuna's side covered her like a wave. She let the arrow slip from her hand and silently fall to the forest floor, its red tether being covered up by leaves. Fighting through the pain, Emuna let out a heartfelt scream.

Brian walked slowly and solemnly back to the caves. Every part of him wanted to go back to Emuna. Every part of him knew he should. But he couldn't, not after what she had said to him, not after how much such a simple sentence had hurt him. There was something he couldn't forget; the tone in her voice. The cold brown eyes that had stared back at him as she threw words she knew would burn. The familiar tone of voice.

The already dark forest seemed even darker. Not even the rays of sun looked like light to him. The darkness of the forest felt as if it was reaching out to Brian and wrapping around his mind, strangling him from the inside out. The wind moaned with its siren call and the trees reached down to grab him.

Brian picked up his pace slightly, not wanting to stay in the woods any longer.

A loud, blood-curdling scream echoed through the forest causing birds to fly off trees and small squirrels to climb into the nearest hole.

Brian paused; his heart skipped a few beats. Perhaps he was imagining things. Perhaps he was wrong. His mind rushed with thoughts, faster than he could grasp them.

With the last of his sanity he held onto an action. Quickly, he began dashing through the forest once again. He ignored his sore arms and legs from the day before and forced himself to press on. His pounding head ache punishing him for every move, breath, and blink.

If he was right. If that scream really was familiar to him. If, in his panicked state, he had still been able to clarify where that scream had come from, then Emuna was in trouble.

With the last of her strength, Emuna fought against the men that held her firmly in their grasps. It was a small fight. The fiery pain in her side kept her at bay and quickly stole her energy from her. The new wound in her side from a sharp dagger caused her to lose more blood than she would like. She gasped for breath that seemed to grow harder to get as the pain grew stronger.

As a last fading hope she closed her eyes and tried to make an orb in her hands that were held behind her back. A small flicker of purple appeared in her hand, but quickly died down. A low chuckle resonated from the Anikulum holding Emuna.

She let out a small yelp and sighed, giving into the pain that covered her body like a blanket of needles. Soon her world grew dark. Then the sound of talking stopped. Entirely unconscious, Emuna was at the mercy of her enemies and without any hope of rescue.

Brian resisted the urge to call Emuna's name lest he give
the enemy his position. He had subconsciously drawn his
sword of light that now pulsed in his hand as he sprinted
through the woods. His breath threatened to grow wavered
and his heart did its best to pump blood to his body
despite its tiring state.

Brian reached an area familiar to him. He had probably
passed this when he went to the hut with Maeve. It looked
recently disturbed, with vines cut down and bushes that
had been trampled on.

Carefully, he tiptoed into the disaster area. A small clink
caught his attention and he looked down to see what he
had stepped on. His breath caught in his throat and the
world seemed to come crashing down on him.

A silver dagger lay on the ground. The blade dripped
with a crimson liquid and the handle broken from a
struggle. The dagger did not glisten, as some do, but,
instead, it was a very solemn piece of metal, seeming to
draw away the light from where it lay.

Brian's sword disappeared. Slowly, he knelt down on
one knee and carefully picked up the dagger. He brushed
his fingers against the blade, the liquid melting onto them
turning his fingers the same bright red. Blood.

Brian felt everything pause, as if he were dreaming.
He held on to the small strand of hope that this wasn't
Emuna's blood, that maybe she had been the one to
draw the blood. Yes, that was it. She had defeated a few

Anikulum, it was their blood he now held on his fingers.

A sudden realization.

She screamed.

She wouldn't scream, not unless she was in trouble...or pain.

Brian's heart ached as he stood up.

"One moment." he said aloud, "I left her for one moment....a single moment."

Brian angrily threw the dagger on the ground and kicked a nearby tree trunk. Everything boiled over and he let out a yell, screaming at the forest for being so blood thirsty. For taking away another person he loved. For no longer being the place of solitude and protection he had been raised to think it was.

No one could make this better, Emuna was hurt, probably dead, and he could do nothing about it. This was his worst nightmare. The very thing he would give his life to avoid. The bane of his being and core of Brian's heart. Helplessness.

Brian jumped when he saw David rushing towards him, a worried look on his face. He reached Brian rather quickly.

"Master Brian." David greeted Brian formally as he looked around for Emuna, "Where is Miss Emuna?" he finally asked.

Brian pointed to the dagger he had so carelessly thrown on the ground. "I heard her scream; I'd left her for just one moment, David! A single moment! She was gone!" Brian said, his voice rising as he spoke.

"Anikulum?" David said.

"I do not know!" Brian yelled, angry at himself for not being there and at David for having to ask.

"All right, we should be going back to the caves. We can...decide what to do then."

Brian nodded silently, part of him wanted to go running after Emuna. To slash through Anikulum until he found her, but a bigger part of him knew that wouldn't be wise. David was right, sadly. Lack of patience is what put Emuna in danger, it was best not to make the same mistake twice.

CHAPTER SIX

INVISIBILITY

"Do you know who I am?" whispered a voice.

Emuna could feel the speaker's cold, wet breath on her neck, but she knew that if she were to turn around there would be nothing. There was nothing, it was all invisible. The tormentor, whoever he was, would not let her see him. She would never know the cause of her death.

"Do you know who I have killed?" the voice continued to taunt, this time in front of Emuna.

Tiredly, she forced herself to respond, "How would I know if I do not know what your face looks like? How am I to know you?" she took a few shallow breaths, "What is it that you want?"

A low chuckle and a strong, forceful punch to her ribs. Emuna let out a yelp as another bone snapped.

"What do I want? What do I want?" the voice said, the sound of footsteps on the floor echoed through the small, dark room as the interrogator continued to taunt and walk behind Emuna. "I want *nothing* you can give me...yet."

What felt like a sharp fingernail ran down Emuna's neck, she fought against it, but could not fight very much. Tied to the small chair in the room, fighting was useless and had proven as such.

The nail stopped halfway down Emuna's neck. The voice made a slight hissing sound and a sharp pain shot through Emuna; she let out a scream as the nail pulled away.

Another chuckle of contented evil, "Scream as you wish. No one can hear you. Your friends have deserted you...or are dead."

An unwarranted tear streamed down Emuna's cheek as she attempted to catch her breath again. "They...would... not...leave me." she gasped out. Her cheeks began to turn a bright red as she cried silently.

"Is that so? It does not appear that you believe that." the voice continued its serenade of endless, heart-breaking taunts. "How may I prove to you that they have left? That you are hopeless. What does faith give you now but a longer death?"

Emuna let out a sob, "Please." she said, "Just kill me and be done. I will not fight."

"No." the voice said flatly, "I have plans for you yet. You are no use to me dead. Though that does not mean you must be in any good condition."

Again came the painful procedures of the many punches and kicks the invisible being would give Emuna.

Brian waited silently in the forest, listening for any sign of human life. The hut that had been the bane of his being for the past day stood in front of him. As he waited for

David's signal he felt his heartbeat rise and his breath quickly began to grow short.

The seconds passed by and Brian began to let his mind wander, his own battle already raging in his mind. *War? Perhaps, but it is war for a reason not for revenge. It is war for Emuna. A reason worth war. But I do not wish to start a war, do I? No, I do not wish to start a war, nor will I. I shall simply go in, get her out quietly, and leave. We will decide what to do from-*

Brian's thoughts stopped when David came from behind him and crouched down next to him. "Are you ready, Master Brian?" David asked hesitantly, already knowing the boy's answer.

Brian nodded, "Most certainly. Let us begin."

David took in a deep breath and whispered a final prayer to Elah. Then he created a bright blue sword in his right hand and that was the signal.

Slowly at first, Brian began to creep out of the forest and towards the hut, attempting to stay in the most concealed corners possible. As he ran along he attempted to make his breathing shallow and quiet.

Soon, he reached the hut door. It was a wood door with two metal bars across the middle. The wood of the door seemed old and chipped and appeared to be decaying. Brian scrunched his nose up at the smell that resonated from it.

After doing a quick look around the area, Brian slowly slid the iron bars out of the door as quietly as possible. When the door was fully unlocked Brian took a deep

breath, created a sword in his left hand and placed his right
hand on the rusted, metal doorknob. He closed his eyes for
a moment and heard his heart beating...once...twice...

"Weak child." the voice taunted Emuna, floating around
her weak form. "Where is your power now? When will
the all-powerful deity save you? Did you not know that he
would forsake you?"

Emuna's breathing was small, almost impossible to
hear or see. Every so often she would gasp as she felt the
fingernail tracing the cut on her neck, but when the feeling
stopped she would close her eyes and resume her semi-
conscious state.

"Faith." the voice scoffed, "Faith they call you. What
faith do you have? Tell me you still have faith! Tell me-"
the voice stopped its taunt and Emuna could hear and feel
it breathing on her neck as it listened. "Footsteps." the
voice growled.

"One of your...guards." Emuna breathed out, "Do you...
fear...your own...men?"

"Shut up!" the voice screamed and, with a gush of wind,
Emuna was unconscious.

Brian heard voices in the hut and quickly came to life. He
swung the door open and rushed inside the dark hut. It
took his eyes a moment to adjust to the pitch blackness
that greeted him. To the right of him, Brian heard a

screeching sound - like the scream of a strange creature, an inhuman, heartless animal - and a loud gust of wind came along with a whispered word.

Agro!

Brian's eyes adjusted just as he started to hear Lupis rushing down the street. His heart skipped a beat when he saw the bound and tortured Emuna in front of him and he began to rush to her, but was suddenly stopped by a Lupi that clamped on his ankle. With a single slice of his sword, the animal was dead, but Brian did not have time to rest before he was attacked by another animal.

Brian fought the army of beasts for a few minutes until it became apparent that he would not be able to save Emuna today. He let out an angered yell as he stabbed a final beast in the heart and created an orb in his hand.

Brian threw the orb at the hut wall and fled through the opening he created. He met up with David and Gavin in the woods and rushed back to the caves, but he left his heart with Emuna, in the dark hut.

When the three men reached the cave they were tired from running, but were glad to seem to have lost the army of creatures awhile back.

Brian walked into the cave, breathing heavily; he sat down on a nearby rock with his elbows resting on his knees and sweat wetting his brow. After catching his breath, he looked up at David, Gavin, and Maeve.

"I was close." he said, "She was right there. She was in front of me."

"We will try again, Master Brian." David reassured, though the disappointment was clear in his voice. "We will not give up. You have my word."

Brian looked down at the ground, "So close."

CHAPTER SEVEN

A CHANGE IN FORM

Emuna hit the ground with a nearly silent thump, her small body making no more than a little sound against the cold, hard stone. She let out a small moan as she heard her shoulder crack.

The cell door shut with a loud clank and she winced at the sound ricocheting around in her head. Her head pounded, her body ached, and she had run out of tears to cry for the life she had lost. This was no life; it never would be.

By now, she had memorized the endless cycle of torture the Anikulum had decided to inflict on her. Everyday she would wake up to the sound of keys as the guard would unlock her prison cell door. They would then grab her and carry her to a small room.

The room would be dark. The only light viewable was through a couple of small cracks in the ceiling where the sun would leak through, attempting to reveal the evil that lay in the shadows. A single chair stood in the middle of the room, one Emuna knew all too well. She would be forced to sit in the chair as they strapped her arms and legs down, preventing her from moving.

Silently, the guards would go about cleaning and re-bandaging her stab wound that was on her side. Their less-than-gentle care of her wound was the only reason she was alive. Why they wished to keep her alive, she did not know. From her point of view, death would be quite enjoyable.

After taking care of her wounds, they would leave her in the room, alone and tormented by her own thoughts. Soon, she would begin to feel sharp pains over her body, cuts would appear on her arms and it would feel as if someone was punching her. Invisible forces left to torture her.

At the end of the day, they would come back into the room and undo her bindings. Roughly, they would carry her nearly lifeless body back to her cell, throw her on the ground, lock the door, and leave her there to prepare for tomorrow, with a small glass of water and, on some days, a piece of bread.

This day was no different. She now lay on the stone floor, alone in a prison cell, in pain, tired, hungry, and quickly growing more weak.

As Emuna lay there, footsteps reached her ears. The annoying tap, tap, tap that came when an Anikulum walked on the cold, stone floor.

The distant sound of footsteps grew louder as they walked closer to her. A small tickle in the back of Emuna's mind wanted her to look up and see who would dare to break the schedule they had set out for her, but she was too weak. Instead, she lay there, still and quiet, unmoving except the small rise and fall of her chest.

A guard appeared at the cell door and fiddled with keys until the door was unlocked. He stepped inside and threw a dark cloak on top of Emuna.

"Put it on." he said in a raspy voice.

Emuna murmured something incoherent and didn't move, in too much pain to think of doing any action.

"I said, put it on." the man growled, his voice low and threatening, "You are one of us now."

Emuna took in a deep breath; her body shuddered with the action. Painfully, she forced herself to sit up straight, becoming nearly paralyzed by the pain that threatened to take her consciousness. She slowly grabbed the cloak.

Until now she had not seen her hands, but now she realized they had become a deathly white. The same hands the Anikulum had. She wondered what her face might look like. She pushed the thought aside for now and proceeded to cover herself with the Anikulum cloak.

Despite the aching pain, Emuna managed to put the cloak on herself, letting a moan of pain escape her lips more than once. Once she was done placing the cloak over her body she resumed her previous position, curled up in a ball on the cold floor. She now quivered with the pain she had awoken.

The guard didn't say anything more. He turned and left, locking the cell door and once again leaving Emuna to her own torments.

"It has been five days." Brian whispered, staring at the grass from his seat on a fallen log. "We have tried three times."

David stopped pacing in front of Brian, hearing the pain in Brian's voice that was threatening to spill over. "I know, Master Brian. Perhaps we haven't tried everything."

Brian looked up, anger mixing in with the sadness in his eyes, "But haven't we? We have tried night and day! Few and many! We could not get her back, David! We are not getting her back!"

David paused for a moment, thinking about his response, "We have not gotten her back yet, but I will die before I give up. Elah would not let her die. He has plans for her yet."

Brian took in a deep breath, trying to calm himself. "Of course, trust in the unseen Elah."

Shockingly, Brian's comment seemed to hurt David, as if he had struck him in the heart.

"You trusted in him when he saved your life! You trusted in him before you knew his name! You trusted in him when you asked to come back to Realta! Do not falter and say you cannot trust in him now, Brian of War! Sometimes, trust is the only line between life and death!" David scolded Brian firmly.

Brian stared up at David for a moment, surprised. David was right. The three of them had grown to trust Elah even more the two months they had stayed in Shamayim. He had become a father to Emuna and a mentor figure to both Brian and Gavin. They were taught that Elah would always help them and that he was there, even when they could not see him. It was hard for Brian to trust someone he did not see when his heart was breaking with every minute that he lived, unsure if Emuna was dead or alive.

Gavin cut in, "Umm... So, we need to get her back, all right?"

David sighed and nodded, "Yes, Sir Gavin. We need to get her back, let us focus on what is before our hands."

Brian shook off David's words and let his mind focus on one thing. "Do we have any more options?"

Gavin looked at David expectantly, waiting for him to mention anything they hadn't tried. Brian went back to staring at the ground.

"There is one more. Something we have not tried. Something that is yet to be tried." David said slowly.

Brian looked up. Gavin listened intently.

"An army of Lumenians, led by Elah himself."

Emuna was being held up by two Anikulum guards. They held her cut and sore arms tightly as they dragged her along, through the run down streets and the dark village. She still wore the black cloak the guard had given her. She kept the hood down, allowing everyone to see her face except herself.

Pain rushed through her body. She would have fought back had she actually had the strength, but she barely managed to stay conscious through the pain, let alone put up a decent fight.

The guards reached an Anikulum that stood a few inches taller than them. He had a sword strapped to his cloak and a broken dagger in his hand, the tip stained with blood. Emuna recognized the dagger and shuddered at the memory.

The guards unceremoniously dropped Emuna on the ground. She landed on her hands and knees, gasping for breath between the pain that shot through her body, reaching to her fingertips. Closing her eyes, she fought back the dizzy spells that began to consume her.

"Emuna of the Wise, is it?" The Anikulum leader asked.

Emuna grimaced and caught her breath just long enough to respond, "Y-yes."

The man chuckled, "You do not seem very wise to me. Which actually works in my favor."

Emuna looked up and glared at the man with the last of the strength she had, her body still quivering.

After a few minutes of staring into the black abyss of the man's cloak, she looked down, unable to stand the darkness that seemed to reach from his cloak and into her heart. Her deepest of all fears hidden in her heart.

The man scoffed, "Defiant, are you? Do not worry, we will get that out of you. You are one of us now."

Emuna fought back the tears of pain stinging at her eyes and forced herself to reply, "O-one of you?... I will never... Be like... You." she said.

"Oh, but you already are."

A bony white hand reached down and gave Emuna an old mirror that appeared to have been in a fire recently.

Reluctantly, she took it. Looking into the reflective surface, she was frightened at what she saw.

Her once beautiful face was now a pale white, her cheeks were sunk in and nearly black circles ran around her eyes. She reached her hand up and gingerly brushed her hair. Her now dark silver hair made her face seem even more white. The only thing left of Emuna were her eyes. The deep, brown eyes that said every emotion before she spoke it. The eyes that now haunted Brian's dreams and showed themselves in every face he saw.

Another chuckle from Anikulum leader, "Do you understand now?"

Emuna dropped the mirror, frightened by her own appearance. "H-how?" she cried, letting a sob escape her mouth as the tears overflowed down her cheeks.

"You chose us, the moment you decided to go against David, the moment you felt resentment in your heart, when you left."

Emuna fell to the ground and buried her face in her arms, crying silently at this new information. The horrible, sad truth that shattered the last of her remaining hope.

"Now, put your hood on, you have work to do."

"Go to Shamayim, find Elah, and tell him everything. Is that clear, Sir Gavin?"

The group of four stood outside of the cave. Gavin held a brown bag packed with a week's worth of supplies, David ran him through their plans once more, and Maeve would pipe up every so often and add a small amount of advice.

Brian listened silently, catching every other word spoken. Something inside him knew Emuna was alive, but a larger something was telling him she was gone. He fought with himself, trying to find the small strand of light in what seemed like an endless, dark tunnel.

"Master Brian?"

Brian snapped out of his daze and looked at David who was staring back at him worriedly.

"Do you wish to bid farewell to Sir Gavin?"

Brian looked at Gavin. Not knowing what else to do, he managed no more than a small nod in the boy's direction, though he knew he deserved more.

Gavin smiled faintly, in an attempt to reassure Brian then turned back to David. "Am I to go on foot?"

David smiled, a joyful smile that hadn't crossed his face since before Emuna's capture. "Of course not, Sir Gavin." Turning to the forest, David let out a low whistle.Silence fell in the woods. Not even the smallest lizard dared to move.

A gush of wind blew the tree tops and a shadow flew through the sky, moving too quickly for any of the watchers to catch the figure of the animal.

Everything remained still and silent for a few more muscle-aching seconds.

Suddenly, a large creature swooped down from the sky, narrowly missing the heads of the travelers and landed a few feet away, barely fitting under the trees.

The creature was a sandy color with wings as white as clouds. It had sharp claws that were filed neatly and kind, bright blue eyes that burrowed into one's soul. It let out a low hum and appeared to have nodded at David, but no one could really tell.

A dragon.

David turned back to Gavin. "His name is Taranis and he will carry you on your journey."

"Taranis?" Gavin repeated, "That is not a name."

David scowled at Gavin, "Do not tease a dragon, young one. You will find he may do more than tease you back."

Gavin took that as a threat and backed off some. "All right...I just...get on top of him?"

David nodded, "He knows where you are going and will stop when you ask him to. Perhaps you will become friends along the way."

Gavin scoffed at becoming friends with an animal and began to timidly walk towards Taranis. Once he reached the dragon's side he placed his hand on the creature's stomach and felt the heat resonating from him. Taranis shifted position and turned his head to watch Gavin with his blue eyes.

Gavin looked into his eyes and shuddered at how deep they seemed, as if they were calling him. Possibly, they were talking to him.

He brushed them off and forced himself to be brave. Fearfully and slowly he climbed onto the dragon's back, hanging onto a harness he found up there. Somebody had harnessed the dragon? And he had let them?

Before Gavin could dwell on that shocking realization, Taranis lifted his wings and took to the skies, almost causing Gavin to fall off.

Once Gavin caught his footing, he looked down and watched as the world rushed by. The town of Realta and all of its worries; gone within an instant.

CHAPTER EIGHT

FORGOTTEN

Emuna walked through the town that was once Realta. Her body still ached from the torture she had received and she tried to avoid bending down and upsetting her stab wound as she went about her daily chores.

After turning into an Anikulum, she had been assigned the job of gathering fire wood. A simple job, at least. Every day she would wake up and be let out of her cell to go about gathering logs of firewood. At the end of the day, she would be given a glass of water and a piece of bread then be taken back to her cell and left there for the night.

Today she went about her normal job, going into the forest, grabbing some logs from the Anikulum forced to chop them, and taking them to any fires that appeared to be dying.

As she walked back to the forest her mind drifted off to her memories. It seemed that the longer she stayed here the harder it was for her to remember anything.

She vaguely remembered meeting a boy. Pondering who the boy was, she began to go through names that he could have gone by, the image of the boy never leaving her mind.

When she reached the edge of the forest, his name finally

came to mind. "Brian." she said out loud, just to feel the name on her lips. The friend she used to know. She wondered if he remembered her. More so, she wondered if he was looking for her.

Brian sat in the cave, staring into the white ashes of what was left of a fire. He hadn't slept more than five hours in a week, but he didn't doze or begin to grow weary as he sat still. No, his mind was going through too many thoughts. He couldn't, no, he wouldn't sleep until Emuna was safe or he had executed his revenge. Retribution for having taken her from him.

He saw Emuna every time he closed his eyes and heard her voice in every ruffle of leaves. She seemed to be haunting him, begging him to rescue her. If only he could. If only-

"Master Brian?"

The same voice woke Brian out of his daze for a countless time that week. David had done a good job of keeping his own emotions hidden. He was the foundation that was keeping Brian's last remaining bit of sanity in the boy's grasp. Without David, Brian would have gotten himself killed by now.

"Lady Maeve wishes for food and I would not mind something either; it has been a few days since we have eaten. Will you come with me?"

Brian sighed and looked up at David. Looking into the soldier's blue eyes, Brian knew that he was not asking a question, but rather stating a command. So Brian nodded and stood up, grabbing his sword just as David began to walk out of the cave.

Emuna walked out of the forest, carrying a small bundle of fire wood. She couldn't carry much due her weak state, but the amount she did carry was enough to feed a fire. Her legs threatened to give out from under her as her mind thought of the pain that covered her body. She was quickly distracted when she heard a familiar voice, even with only half of her memories, she knew this voice. She would never forget it.

"Tristen!" Emuna shouted, dropping the logs she held and ignoring them as they fell to the ground with a loud thump.

An Anikulum a few feet away turned to Emuna. The dark hood he wore covered his eyes, but Emuna could feel his cold glare staring into her soul.

She ignored the feeling and ran up to the man, embracing him in a hug. Her hood fell off her, but she payed no heed to it.

The Aniklumun grunted and angrily pushed Emuna away.

"What are you doing?" he scolded, crossing his arms over his chest, seeming not to notice her face.

"Emuna?" she said, realizing the shocking truth too late, "Y-your sister....I'm Emuna.... Tri...Tristen?"

"Who are you talking about?" the man asked roughly.

Emuna paused, running through her options. She had to

know, she had to find a way to remind him. As a last resort, she reached up and pushed the man's hood off his head. She felt her heart go to her throat and held her breath.

She wasn't looking at the face of her brother, but the face of monster. He had gone entirely pale, his face was thin, and his once kind, brown eyes were now entirely black. His eyes glared back, a heart wrenching scowl from someone she had once loved so much.

"Idiot!" he yelled, shoving Emuna.

She fell to the ground and let out a yell in pain.

"Never touch me again!" Tristen said, covering his face with his hood once more.

Emuna looked up at him, tears imminent in her eyes. "Please, brother...please." she begged, holding back the sobs of heartbreak that wished to leave her.

"Do not call me that." Tristen commanded, "I may have been your brother once, I cannot remember, but I am no one's brother now. Now, carry on with your work or I will tell someone superior to me." Tristen turned and walked away, leaving Emuna sitting on the ground

Emuna's body shook with a sob and she let the tears fall from her eyes, ignoring the pile of wood she had dropped and her job. She gave up; she wanted to die. If this would be her life from now on then she would rather not have a life. As a last fading hope she called out to the only person she thought might hear her.

"I'm sorry." she whispered between sobs, "Elah, I'm sorry. Please, save me. Take my life if you must, but free me, please."

Two rough hands reached down and grabbed Emuna, forcing her to stand despite the sharp, tear-inducing pain that rushed through her body. She let out a moan of objection, but other than that she put up no fight.

The man holding her dragged her down the street. He mumbled a few words she barely understood, "Do not ever speak that name again."

Emuna closed her eyes as she was dragged along, trying to forget the shooting pain that occurred with every small movement. Soon, her breath began to come in small gasps and she struggled to control it.

By the time the man reached her cell Emuna was half-conscious and her eyes were nearly closed. The guard threw her into the cell, causing more pain to overflow. She let out a scream that echoed through the prison.

The guard backed away slightly, seeming frightened by Emuna. Hurriedly, he locked the cell and rushed out.

Emuna lay still and silent, recovering from her trauma. Her heart beat was her only company in the dark, damp cell that would be the death of her if she did not get out soon. With her rhythmic beating, Emuna went entirely unconscious, surrendering to the nightmares that would now torture her.

Brian watched silently, every bone in his body wanted to lunge out of the forest when he saw Emuna's hood fall. He saw her eyes, the deep, brown eyes he thought he would never see again. In an attempt to keep himself at bay he closed his eyes and turned away, leaving David watching by himself.

He heard the words of Emuna's brother scolding her and the yell of pain she had let out; he wondered what had pained her. The worse, by far the most painful thing, was knowing he had to wait. Brian could not go rushing in and scoop Emuna in his arms, happy she was alive. He had to wait. And wait he did, even if it broke his heart more than thinking she was dead.

When Emuna was out of sight, David turned back to Brian, sorrow in his face. "I am sorry." was the only words he managed to speak.

Brian opened his eyes and looked up, glaring at David. "You knew, didn't you? You knew she would become one of them! Why didn't you tell me?"

David seemed taken aback by Brian's question, but he composed himself and answered in a normal tone, much more quiet than Brian's. "I had my suspicions. I hoped I was wrong, but this expedition has proved me right, sadly."

Brian looked away from David's remorseful eyes and stared at a nearby leaf. "When will Gavin return?"

"Two days."

"Then we have to wait two more days," Brian looked back at David, tears stinging at his eyes, though he held them back, "I will wait *only* until then."

CHAPTER NINE

A LURKING ENEMY

Birds chirped songs in the far distance as Gavin quietly walked through the forest, his feet making little to no sound on the leafy, forest floor. He held a throwing dagger in his hand as he scanned the forest for any animal he could use for food.

He had been traveling for about twelve hours. After landing in Antrum - the forest after the Northern Mountains - Gavin had left Taranis in an opening in the trees. How the dragon had managed to fit in the forest without his head towering over the tree tops was a wonder to Gavin.

As the boy walked through the forest he heard a loud explosion-like sound, followed shortly by a cry from a girl. He jumped, startled for a moment. As quickly and quietly as he could, he walked towards the direction in which he had heard the cry.

Soon, he reached the edge of the forest, but there was no girl. As he looked around, he saw no sign of human life.

A slither of fear began to crawl up Gavin's back and he shuddered at its cold memory. He slowly backed away from the forest edge and started making his way back towards Taranis. Gavin hoped that, even if his companion was just a dumb beast, he would protect him.

It took Gavin a few minutes of walking through the forest to find where he had decided to camp. Taranis had apparently started a fire and he now sat comfortably beside it, his light blue eyes staring into the red flames.

Gavin sat down a few feet beside the dragon. To his surprise, Taranis pushed, with his paw, a large bundle of fruit towards Gavin, then rested his head on his paws and watched the boy closely.

Gavin looked from the fruit to the animal, wondering what he should do. Hesitantly, he took an apple from the bundle and began to eat it.

Taranis made a slight rumbling sound in the back of his throat and turned away from Gavin, intently staring at the fire once again.

"Did you hear that sound?" Gavin asked the animal, unsure why he had suddenly decided to strike up a conversation with a dragon.

Taranis lifted his head and looked questionably at Gavin.

"No...of course you didn't." Gavin said slowly, "You probably don't even understand what I am speaking of." Gavin angrily threw the apple on the ground.

Taranis growled angrily.

"What? I was done with it!" Gavin said.

Taranis let out a huff of air and turned back around. He curled up in a small ball - well, small for a creature of his size anyways - and went to sleep, paying no heed to the worried and frightened boy that sat behind him.

The two days Brian had promised to wait seemed as if they were ages to him. For two days he saw nothing but Emuna's eyes, her pale face, and her silver hair. He wondered if this was what Emuna had gone through when searching for her family. He wondered why he did not worry for his own family; his father and his mother. Why he did not wish to find them.

As the hours ticked by and the day grew darker, David also grew more concerned. Though his concern was not for Emuna, but for Brian. The young boy had quickly grown more tired and restless and he worried that he might attempt a dangerous act to get the girl back.

During the evening hours, David sat beside Brian who sat on a boulder, carving away at a stick. David cleared his throat, attempting catch the boy's attention.

Brian paused, but did look up from his work. "Yes?" he said quietly, his voice nearly a whisper.

"We will save her, Master Brian." David said slowly.

Brian sighed, "How can you be so sure?"

"Because it is not her time to die."

Gavin flinched and sat up, quickly waking from his light sleep. He blinked a few times as his eyes adjusted to the darkness of night.

Taranis was already awake and stood beside Gavin, his paw barely touched the boy as he too listened to the night.

Gavin could not see Taranis's eyes, but he knew the dragon was also watching. Something was close, it lurked in the distance and the animal knew it.

Taranis made a small sneezing sound and blew a puff of smoke out. He then took in a deep breath and blew it out quickly. In a simple breath he lit up the forest with a quick burst of fire. For a moment, the scenery was as clear as day.

Gavin's eyes grew wide as he saw the huge army that was hiding in the bushes, about to attack. He placed his hand on his sword hilt and drew it quickly, preparing himself for a fight.

Taranis growled deep in his throat and swayed his tail back and forth, his unease clearly showing. Slowly, he began to show his teeth in a menacing snarl, as if he were daring the army to attack.

A small flicker of light came from the forest, like a spark of a fire being started, but it vanished more fast than lightning.

Taranis suddenly grabbed Gavin in his mouth and put him on his back. As the army began to charge from the woods the dragon spread his wings and flew into the sky, traveling almost too fast to see.

Gavin hung onto Taranis's harness tightly; he turned around to see the forest as they narrowly escaped. His hands almost slipped, when the shock of what he saw hit him.

A large black orb began to grow from the forest, covering the entire clearing Gavin and Taranis had stayed the night in. Suddenly, the black light turned gray.

Taranis turned suddenly, causing Gavin to look away just as an explosion sounded behind them.

When Gavin looked back, the forest was silent as dust settled on the freshly burned trees.

"I've heard that noise before." Gavin said thoughtfully.

CHAPTER TEN

A KIND OF FREEDOM

Gavin slipped off Taranis's back and landed on the soft, green grass. It was a bright day and the sun shined down on the town of Shamayim as if it were smiling at it. Birds sang in the distance and white clouds sprinkled the light blue sky.

Taranis stretched his wings and shook away the long flight. They had reached Shamayim about two days after they left Realta. Now it was up to Gavin to alert Elah of their pressing issue.

Hurriedly, Gavin rushed through the many tents and roads of Shamayim. Soon he reached Elah's tent. It was a white tent with intricate designs decorating the edges of it.

The wind blew open the doorway and Gavin ducked inside. He now stood in a large tent, wonderfully furnished and meant for royalty. A table was in the middle of the tent and two men stood over it, intently studying what appeared to be a map.

Gavin went over to the table.

"Good Sirs, I have come to see Elah. Where might I find him this hour?" Gavin addressed the men formally, putting all his training as the chief's son together to sound as sophisticated as he could.

The man with brown hair and brown eyes looked up from the map while the other man kept staring intently at the paper. "He is not here. You are misinformed if you think you could find him here."

"I assure you, I am not misinformed. Do you think your information could be wrong?" Gavin said slowly.

"No, I am certain he is not here. He said he was going on a journey...and that he would not return."

Gavin's eyes widened, "Wh-what? No, you can't be right! He has to be here somewhere!" he suddenly screamed, panic setting in.

The other man looked up from the map and spoke calmly, "We knew this time would come, boy. Take it in stride. Go back to your home, everything will work out in time."

Gavin paused, "What do you mean 'we knew this time would come'?" he questioned, "Elah has been preparing for a journey for awhile? Did he tell you something?"

The two men exchanged shocked glances and turned back to Gavin, the brown-haired one spoke. "You do not know of the prophecy?"

Gavin shook his head.

Emuna leaned against the cell wall, asleep. She had cried herself to sleep after sobbing silently for a few hours. Her hood was no longer on her and her face was clearly visible. Besides the gentle rise and fall of her chest, she made no other movement; though her lack of movement was not to be mistaken as a peaceful sleep. Dreams flew around her mind and tormented her even in her slumber.

As she slept the streams of light that strained to reach inside her dark cell began to circle around her. The light soon covered her skin, causing her to glow a light color. Her silver hair began to change color and slowly melted back into her dark brown hair.

An Anikulum guard walked up to Emuna's cell. He cowered a little as he watched the girl being covered by the strands of light. Her pale skin began to change color as the light sank into her.

With one final blast the light shot through the cell, nearly blinding the guard. Then everything was back to darkness.

Emuna still lay in a deep rest on the cell floor. Her skin had returned to its tan shade. The cuts on her arms and her stab wound looked as fresh as the days they had been made, some even bled, but she was no longer Anikulum. She was Lumenian and she would remain Lumenian. Even in her weakened state she seemed to glow with a power the Anikulum did not possess.

The guard stood, startled, for a moment, but forced himself to push it aside. Quietly, he unlocked the cell door and walked inside, roughly picking Emuna up.

She gasped, awoken from her nightmare, and opened her eyes. Once she realized that she was simply being dragged off again she began to drift back off into sleep. Secretly wishing they would simply kill her and be done.

The guard shook Emuna hard, causing her to wake.

"No sleeping." he commanded in his gravelly voice as he dragged her through the many cells.

Emuna forced herself to stay awake. She kept her mind busy by looking into the cells. Most of them were empty, besides the occasional one that held a sleeping and tortured Anikulum. Emuna's heart sunk for the captives; if she could get them out, she would.

As the guard dragged her by the last cell she saw something that shocked her.

Elah stood in the cell, his skin glowed a small amount, though hardly seeable. He had a sad expression on his face and Emuna thought she may have seen sparkling tears in his eyes.

Emuna opened her mouth to call to him, but nothing came out. A spell of silence only able to be cast by David and Elah himself. But why would Elah silence her? Why wouldn't he let her save him? She began to panic. She had grown to love Elah more than she had realized and seeing him in one of the same cells she had been tortured in sent a wave of new pain through Emuna. The last of her heart breaking.

Once the guard reached the prison door, Emuna gathered her strength and let out a heartfelt scream, breaking the spell that had been cast upon her voice.

The guard startled and nearly dropped Emuna, but managed to catch her. He grunted angrily at Emuna, but did not hit her. Though Emuna was certain he would. The guard then pulled her to the edge of the forest and dropped her by a patch of bushes. He stared at the quivering and frightened girl for a second before turning and walking away.

Emuna blinked, shocked. A million questions rushed through her head as her now fresh wounds knocked on her consciousness. She began to feel dizzy and barely fought back the sleep that was calling her.

Had the guard just set her free? Why? She could not believe that she had just been released from the captivity she had been in, free from the torture that was so intently forced upon her.

Painfully, she forced herself to stand, using a nearby tree to lift herself up. She grunted as her muscles moved along and she walked into the forest. Her mind focused on one thing, getting back to the caves. If she could just get back to the caves she could find Brian and he would help her.

Brian. She remembered him now. She remembered Brian, David, Gavin, and Maeve. How she had forgotten them was beyond her knowledge, but she was glad she remembered them. They would help her, if she could just get within ear shot. If she didn't pass out from pain first.

Emuna struggled through the forest, taking gasping breaths as she forced herself forward. Her legs shook with pain and her arms ached. She could feel her heart beating along with her migraine and she grimaced at the pain.

"This is not freedom." she whispered, saying her thoughts out loud. "It is a kind of freedom, but no true freedom comes at the price of another...why...why did Elah stay there?"

She paused in her walk, holding her stab wound that proceeded to stain her hands red. Something inside Emuna knew the answer to her question, though she didn't know how.

"He...he...wanted to save me."

She placed her hand on a nearby tree and steadied herself, trying to keep from passing out. Though, despite her efforts, sleep was becoming more difficult to fight as the pain grew harder to ignore. Giving up on her seemingly useless battle with rest, Emuna sunk to the ground and let her eyes fall closed. Drifting off into another nightmare-filled slumber.

Brian stood in the middle of a large forest. He looked around slowly. The forest was still as the streams of daylight made their way through the canopy. A gentle fog covered the ground and circled around Brian's feet. He was almost lethargic with the calm and serenity of the forest. Due to his nearly-asleep state, he jumped when a voice called to him.

"Brian." came the gentle voice of Elah, "Come to the forest. Emuna awaits your rescue. Come to the forest."

Brian awoke with a jolt, sweat streamed down his forehead. Quickly, he grabbed his sword and stood up.

David woke up instantly when he heard the noise of Brian awakening. He sat up in bed just in time to see the boy rush out of the cave. Hurriedly, he stood up and chased after him.

Emuna jumped and woke up, opening her eyes too fast for her migraine which resumed its endless pounding. She moaned and closed her eyes again, but then remembered she needed to get to Brian. Even if her entire body protested her every breath.

So, slowly and with much effort, Emuna managed to use a tree to help her stand up. She took in a deep breath to steady her breathing and pushed herself onward in the direction she hoped was the caves.

Emuna walked for about ten minutes before stopping, she couldn't go on, it was too much. She leaned against a tree, trying to keep herself standing. Her breathing was shallow and she could feel herself sinking to the ground, slowly slipping into unconsciousness.

Brian saw Emuna leaning on a tree though a patch of bushes. Before David put together what was happening, Brian dashed forward, reaching Emuna just as she began to slip to the ground.

"Emuna?" he whispered, gently wrapping his arms around her to keep her standing. "What happened?" Brian felt the cuts on her arms and saw the blood on her shirt from her wounded side.

Emuna mumbled something incoherent and kept her eyes closed, too tired to do anything more.

Brian sighed and carefully picked up Emuna. She rested her head on his shoulder as he began to walk back towards the caves, David following close behind.

Soon, Emuna drifted off into a deep sleep. A dreamless, lovely sleep.

CHAPTER ELEVEN

LIFE AND DEATH

Brian carried Emuna back to the caves. He did his best to cover his emotions as he watched Maeve tend to her many wounds. After the grueling process of cleaning and bandaging her cuts was done, David left the cave to find some food. Judging by the amount of weight Emuna had lost, she would be very hungry when she woke up.

Now Brian sat next to the sleeping Emuna. He held a dagger and piece of wood in his hands and expertly carved away at the wood. Maeve sat a few feet away, quietly watching Brian.

Silence filled the cave and wrapped around Maeve and Brian. Neither of them had spoken since David left. Maeve thought that there was so much to say, yet no way to start . So they sat still, neither of them speaking, waiting for something to happen.

The moon hung high in the sky as midnight reared closer. Darkness shrouded over the forest and rain drops began to fall freely down to the ground. Lightning flashed and struck a tree in the forest, thunder rumbled in response.

The whole world seemed to weep on this dark night. A great event was to take place tonight.

Elah stood under a tree, his hands and legs bound with rope. His face was bruised and his kind, brown eyes expressed despair. A rope with a slip knot was hanging on his neck as he stared silently into the throng of Anikulum before him.

The evil race of creatures gathered around him, being sure to stay out of reach of him because even bound and nearing death he was still more powerful than them all. They watched with wide eyes as the last adjustments were made to the boulder that would drop and pull the string tightly around Elah's neck, ending his life.

Only one man stood close enough to touch Elah, if he reached out his hand his fingertips would barely brush Elah's arm. Though, it was not out of bravery that the man stood close to Elah, but out of the coldness of his heart. He wanted to be as close as he could, to make sure Elah breathed his last breath.

This particular man wore a long cloak, like the Anikulum, but his hands were that of human or Lumenian. They were not pale and looked strong. His face was not visible behind the shadow the cloak, but somehow it was possible to feel it. In an onlooker's mind, they could see the man's face, with jet black hair and eyes darker than a starless night. The image would send shivers up one's back.

As the last of preparations were made for Elah's execution, the man watched. Everything stilled. The crowd dared not to make even the smallest of sounds. Silently, the man lifted his hand. Then, he dropped it down quickly, it landed on his side, ruffling his cloak.

An Anikulum guard pushed a boulder, connected to Elah by some rope, off the tree. The boulder plummeted down until it reached the end of the rope. It stopped and hung in mid-air, rain drops pelting its smooth surface.

Emuna woke to a bright flash of light followed shortly by a loud rumble of thunder. She lay still for a moment until another crash of thunder shot through the air and caused her to open her eyes. Emuna stirred slightly, but stopped when she felt how sore she was from her recent ordeals.

Her mind wandered to what she was doing in a cave. As she looked around and realized the ashes of a fire and two forms sleeping in front of her, she remembered. She let out a sigh of relief, happy to be safe for now.

"Master Brian has finally fallen asleep." David whispered, startling Emuna for a second. He sat down in front of her. "How are you feeling?"

Emuna relaxed and forced herself to sit up. "I am better, I suppose."

David smiled faintly, "That is good. Master Brian will be happy to hear that when he wakes."

"He fell asleep?" Emuna asked.

"Yes," David said, "He has not slept a great deal since you have been gone. I would wake him, if only he did not deserve three hours rest."

Emuna looked down, suddenly remembering how she had come to be set free. She took in a deep breath, forcing herself to ask the question that hung in her mind. "David?" she whispered, her voice sounding little and frightened, like that of a child.

"Yes?" David said, coaxing Emuna forward.

"Elah was there...I think...I think he traded himself for me."

David sighed, "Yes."

"Why?"

"When-"

"Emuna, you're awake!" Brian said, neither David nor Emuna had realized he'd woken up, but he didn't seem to care.

He walked, or rather ran, to Emuna. Before he had time to think better of it he had Emuna embraced in a strong, but gentle hug. She didn't object, she'd missed Brian more than she had realized.

"I am sorry..." she mumbled into his shoulder, holding back tears. "I did not mean what I said. I am sorry, I was terrible, Brian. I am sorry."

Brian pulled away, keeping his hands on her arms, he smiled faintly. "It is fine. You are back; that is all that matters." he said, nearly a whisper.

Emuna shook her head, "I knew it would hurt you, I am sorry. You told me such things in trust, I am-"

"Emuna." Brian said, gently brushing away a strand of hair from her eyes. "I am fine. I am just happy you are back. You do not have to apologize, all right?"

Emuna nodded and went back to burying her head in

Brian's chest, trying to hide her teary eyes from everyone. Brian held her closely. He wasn't going to lose her again.

Gavin sat next to the table in Elah's tent, awestruck and speechless. The two men looked at him and waited for his reaction to the tale they'd told. It took a few minutes, but Gavin finally regained his speech.

"He is going to die?" he said slowly, trying to make sense of everything.

The men nodded.

"But...he isn't *really* going to die...right?"

"Gavin, we already told you. He is going to die, but he will be back." one of the men said.

"He is going to be back?"

"Yes." the other man said.

"And by dying he will...he will save the humans and Anikulum?"

The men nodded, "If the Anikulum is the unknown race spoken of in the prophecy. Then, yes. The humans and the Anikulum."

Gavin sighed, "Very well...though, I wish he did not have to die."

One of the man smiled, "He will live again, young soldier. Though, for now, it seems you have the more pressing issue. Tell us of this girl you were sent to save."

CHAPTER TWELVE

THE WRONG INFORMATION

It was a bright and sunny day in the town of Shamayim. The birds sang their daily songs and the occasional bright yellow bumblebee would buzz by on its way to a nearby flower. Everything seemed calm and serene, from the blue sky to the gentle breeze.

Gavin sat atop Taranis. The dragon kept his wings down and pressed against his sides so the boy could see the man talking to him. Gavin nodded in understanding as the soldier explained to him, once again, the message he was to deliver to David. With a final goodbye, the man backed away to give room for the dragon to fly away. Gavin held onto the dragon's harness, used to the take off by now.

With a swift movement of his wings the dragon took the skies. A strong wind blew Gavin's hair and nearly made him fall off, but he held on tightly.

After a few minutes of silence Gavin began to grow weary, his eyes drooped with fatigue and his hands slipped from the harness. Taranis swerved a small amount, jolting Gavin from his sleep.

"Hey!" Gavin scolded as he held onto the harness tightly, "Do not do that!"

Taranis blew out a puff of smokey air in protest, then he did something Gavin did not expect, "You are the one that fell asleep. Of all the egotistical, narcissistic things to do. Fall asleep while riding a dragon may be one of the dumbest I have seen yet." came the deep voice of the dragon.

Gavin paused and stared wide eyed at the harness he held onto tightly. He hardly noticed when the dragon turned around to look at him through his deep blue eyes. "You talked!" he blurted out, as if the animal had not obviously vocalized.

"Of course I talked." Taranis said, his mouth did not open, but sound did indeed come from it.

Gavin stared at the dragon, in shock. Finally, he recovered his voice, "Why have you not talked before?"

"Because I was deciding whether or not you were worth talking to." Taranis turned back to looking ahead as he spoke.

"Of course I'm worth talking to I-"

Gavin's voice was cut off by the familiar voice of David, "Gavin, Taranis, come down! I wish to speak with you!" it called from the ground that was unseeable due to a thick fog.

Taranis stopped going forward and hovered in one spot, careful to make sure his wings made no noise.

"Well, you heard him. Land." Gavin said impatiently.

Taranis snorted a small flame in response, "What if it is not David?" he asked.

"Who else would it be?" Gavin taunted, "Pavix? Just land."

90

Taranis slowly began to float to the ground, "It would be best if you do not use that name as if it were a common word." he said cautiously just as his feet touched the ground.

It was not the bright and happy day it had been when they left Shamyim. Instead, the world now had a sinister and evil essence, as if it were trying to swallow Gavin and Taranis up and use them for its own wicked deeds. Fog covered the ground making it difficult to see more than a few feet ahead and dark clouds covered the sun and kept light from reaching the ground.

Taranis shifted uncomfortably under Gavin, unsure of his new surroundings. He felt as if darkness was crawling up his back, trying to strangle him.

Gavin felt the same and he unconsciously held tighter to Taranis' harness. He felt the panic welling in his throat, but he pushed it away and forced himself to stay still.

Soon, a silhouette began to come into view. The man seemed to be about the same height and body shape as David.

The silhouette stopped growing a few feet away from the dragon and the boy.

It was impossible to see any of the facial features on the man and, therefore, Gavin and Taranis were left guessing that this man must be David.

"Gavin, it is good to know you are all right." came David's voice over the thick fog.

"Yes..." said Gavin hesitantly, "Why would I not be?"

"The Anikulum..."

"What about them?"

"They found the caves in Realta, attacked Emuna, Brian,

and me. I was able to get free, but the other two were taken by Pavix. Nobody knows what he will do to them."

Gavin felt a small spark of panic rise in him, but he quickly pushed it away, "What about Lady Maeve?"

There was a pause before David answered. "She passed..." David's voice grew solemn, "Dead."

Gavin's heart sunk, "What should I do?"

Gavin felt Taranis tense underneath him, as if the question was not something good to ask.

"You must go on another journey." said David, "Go deep into the uncharted territories, until you come across Pavix's castle, you will know it when it is in view."

Gavin nodded, but he did not know if David could see him, "When should I go?" he asked.

"Now."

"Now?" repeated Gavin.

"Yes, now. You do not have much time. I have wasted enough telling you of this event. You must go. Now."

Gavin hesitated, but felt Taranis prepare to set off into the skies once again.

"Now!" David commanded a final time and for a moment Gavin thought it did not sound like David's voice.

Taranis jumped from the raised tone of voice then quickly shot into the sky, leaving the fogged ground behind. The dragon disappeared behind a cloud as he headed deeper into the uncharted territories.

The silhouetted form of David stood still for a moment, until it began to change. It morphed and seemed to melt into a different figure. This one was taller than David and had longer, unkempt, hair. This man's hands were set into tight fists, one wrapped around the hilt of a sword that was strapped to his side.

He stood there, staring into the sky at the spot where the dragon had vanished. The only thing visible were the eyes. Black eyes. No light could be seen in the sinister darkness that surrounded them.

Emuna woke up slowly and resisted the urge to adjust her sleeping position as she was still sore. She opened her eyes a small amount, being greeted by bright, morning sunlight for the first time since she'd come back to Realta. Her dark brown eyes searched her surroundings.

Brian sat a few feet to the right of her. He twirled an arrow in his right hand and kept a steady stare at the small fire pit in the middle of the cave. His shoulders slumped and he leaned on his legs. The usually tidy hair he kept was tangled and his normally alert eyes seemed to be drifting to another place.

Emuna cleared her throat, almost a hum, as she slipped her hands underneath herself and sat up.

Brian turned to face her. His lips spread into a thin smile, but his eyes remained tired and lifeless, as if he had come out of a fire and was still lost, filled with nightmares of his tormented mind.

"Good morning." he whispered, trying not to wake David or Maeve since they both slept on the ground in the cave. "Are you feeling better?"

Emuna nodded her head, her eyes unmoving from Brian's as she tried to understand what could be going through his mind.

"That is good." The arrow stilled in Brian's hand. "It is good to know you are getting better."

Emuna let out a gentle sigh and forced herself to stand up. She walked, or rather limped, over to where Brian stood. Brian watched her, his body tensed. When she reached Brian, Emuna began to sink to the ground. Brian's gentle hands caught her and he helped her to sit down beside him.

"You should not be walking yet." Brian said.

"Do you have another means of transportation?" Emuna said, a small twinkle in her eyes. "Besides, I wanted to sit beside you."

Brian let a smile cross his face, "Very well, but you should not make a habit out of it."

Emuna did not respond. She let silence fill the room for a moment as she thought, Brian still cautiously watching her.

"Do you think what David said is true?" she asked, breaking the pause in the conversation.

"About what?" Brian asked.

"About...Elah...you know, coming back."

Brian thought for a moment, "I would hope so."

Emuna sighed, "Me too."

CHAPTER THIRTEEN

RETURNING FROM DEATH

Emuna sat in the middle of the cave, eating a rabbit
that David had caught and cooked for her. Hungrily, she
scooped the food into her mouth, not speaking a word.
Her only sustenance while in captivity had been bread and
water, this food was beyond food to her. It was freedom.

Brian sat beside her, carving at another piece of wood. His
hands were steady and strong as he carved intricate details into
the item, hardly noticing anything else. Of all Brian's many
talents, carving was the one he did the most and by far the most
extraordinary one. He did not say where he had learned it or why
he always carved when he was in any form of emotional distress,
but then again, nobody asked him.

David and Maeve were talking on the other side of the
cave. Emuna and Brian did not seem to be interested in
their whispered conversation and both carried on with their
activities.

Once Emuna was done eating she looked up to see Brian
putting the finishing touches on his carving. She watched
patiently as his knife expertly slipped over the carving
material, taking a small amount off with each stroke.

Brian caught Emuna watching him out of the corner of his eye and he looked up. He smiled at her kindly.

"What are you making?" Emuna asked, unable to see the entirety of the sculpture as Brian held it in his hands.

Brian handed the wood to Emuna. She took it carefully and studied it as Brian re-sheathed his dagger and attached it to his belt.

The sculpture was smooth and refined. She now held the wooden figure of a young girl. The girl's hair went down to her waist, just slightly longer. She wore a long dress with a scarf that almost seemed to be swaying when the sculpture was moved. Her eyes looked up into Emuna. Big, almond-shaped eyes that stared into the soul. Emuna's eyes.

"Do you like it?" Brian asked, unconsciously fumbling with his thumbs as Emuna ran her fingers over his sculpture.

Emuna stilled her hands and simply looked at the beautiful carving, "Is it me?" she whispered, not looking up.

"Yes." He said, "Is that all right? I can burn it if you want. I just wanted to-"

Emuna looked up, smiling, the joy in her eyes silencing Brian. "Yes, it is fine. I really like it," she let out a small laugh and looked back down at the sculpture, "I guess I lost the pegasus in the Northern Mountains' caves."

"I can make you another one," he said, "It is not much work. I enjoy it, anyways."

She looked back up, locking eyes with Brian. "Why do you enjoy carving these sculptures so much?"

Brian seemed to turn pale and he looked away suddenly,

staring at the fire intently as if it were the most interesting thing in the world.

Before Emuna could say something David spoke up.

"Do you two mind coming with me for a walk?" he asked from across the cave, "If Miss Emuna is feeling strong enough to walk, of course."

Taranis flew a few miles before landing in a large field. The fog had lifted and no longer shrouded his vision and the blue sky was once again visible. Everything was as it should be.

Gavin slipped off Taranis's back and walked in front of him, looking the dragon in the eyes. "What did you stop for?" he said, "Do you not understand? My friends are in danger! We need to go help them!"

"I do not think they are in danger." Taranis said, swishing his tail back and forth as he stretched his wings. "I also do not think that was David. And I certainly do not think we should stray from our path to follow an unknown source."

"Of course that was David!" Gavin protested, "Who else would it be?"

Taranis growled deep in his throat. He bent his neck down, his face just inches away from Gavin's now. The dragon stared intently at the boy. "Evil trying to be mistaken for good."

Gavin took a half step back, "It was David." he said, "And I am going, with or without your approval."

Taranis was about to respond, but Gavin turned and

began to walk away, in the northern direction. Taranis sighed and walked next to the boy, but did not look down at him. "Then I am going with you, to be sure you are protected."

The small group walked through the forest for an hour before Emuna begged for a rest and they stopped. They were now deep into the forest, trees and vines surrounded them. In order to take a few steps forward they would have to cut down vines.

David had created a small opening in the thick greenery where Emuna now sat on a boulder. Brian stood beside her, checking her many cuts to make sure she had not injured herself further.

David looked around the forest, his eyes scanning the trees intently. His hand rested on his sword hilt, though he was not tense as one would think, but quite relaxed. He stood stone still, making no noise. Listening. Waiting.

Brian caught the glimpse of a figure out of the corner of his eye. He stood up and drew his sword in one fluid motion. Emuna tensed, her hands getting a small purple tinge to them.

"David," Brian said, "Did you see that?"

David remained calm. Brian could hear the smile in his voice. "Yes I did, Master Brian."

After a few moments of silence the bushes to the right of David began to move. A hand reached out of the bushes and pushed them aside, revealing the man Brian had seen.

He had dark, chocolate brown hair. His eyes, no word

could describe their depth, seemed to show a million emotions at once; eyes that looked into the future, eyes that had seen the past, eyes that somehow found their way back to the present. His neck had a red, thin scar that ran around it, other than this there was no other blemish about him. For he was perfect both inside and out.

"Elah." Emuna whispered from behind Brian and David, as if his presence had to be confirmed. She gathered herself quickly and stood up. Stumbling, Emuna managed to walk over to the man.

She was tired and her legs were shaking, but something compelled her further. A force stronger than her weakness held her up.

Brian and David remained quiet as they watched what transpired between Emuna and Elah. They knew it was not their place to talk yet.

"Is it really you?" Emuna asked, standing in front of Elah, her eyes wide with intrigue and surprise.

Elah nodded, "Yes, it is me." his voice came out like a song and flew around Emuna's ears, soothing her soul.

Emuna lifted a shaking hand to his neck. She carefully brushed her fingers against his scar, silently envisioning what could have taken place. A single tear streaked down her cheek, landing on the forest floor without a sound.

Elah sighed, "There is no need for tears, daughter." he said, "My life was not given in vain, nor do I return to life without a cause. Though I did die for you, I died also for thousands more. One life to save many. A flawless, eternal life."

Emuna looked up from his scar and into his eyes. She took in a deep breath and shuddered. "So...the h-human race...they are free?"

"They are free," Elah said, "You are free. Even the Anikulum that choose my love are free. But, sadly, there are still things amiss in our world, for it will not be perfect for many centuries. You, my children, Brian, Emuna, and Gavin - who is currently away - shall be my soldiers of war. I shall use you as my hand and you shall be my tools. Together, we can set things right, as they once were."

Brian stepped forward, so he was right behind Emuna and close enough to touch Elah. "What can we do, Sir?" he asked.

"Much, but I have not come to discuss the future with you but the present. Gavin is heading back from Shamayim to your knowledge, yes?"

Brian nodded.

"Then I must inform you of what has come to past." Elah said, "Gavin has been deceived by Pavix. He believes that Emuna and Brian were captured by the Anikulum and are being taken deep into the lands beyond Shamayim to Pavix's castle. He has turned around and is heading into a trap far worse than you can imagine."

"When did this happen?" David asked, his voice no longer calm and collected as it had been.

"Less than a day ago, but it has already been too long." Elah said, "All of you must go to save him, soon. Come, let us go to the caves. We will be safer there and I think there is somebody waiting to meet Emuna once all is explained."

Elah smiled and gently took Emuna's hand, leading her back into the forest. Brian and David followed close behind.

CHAPTER FOURTEEN

A HAUNTING PAST

Maeve was unsure whether to be shocked, frightened, or overjoyed to see Elah. When she first saw him she did little else than look at him, studying his every feature and deciding for herself whether or not to believe in him, to trust an unknown person that claimed to be a divine being.

After a few minutes of being around Elah and some prodding from David, Maeve had grown to accept this change in her world. That there was indeed a god in existence. Someone that watched and knew everything. The "I" in the ancient scrolls, an immutable, eternal, all-knowing being that cared for everyone. The very person everybody wished they had in their life. A friend, father, brother, and mentor.

"All of you are just going to leave?" Maeve said skeptically after being told of Gavin's mistake and the other's plan to go after him. "You have only just arrived, the village is overrun by Anikulum, and what of the ones that have been captured?"

David spoke first, "We have no choice but to leave. We must stop Sir Gavin and there is only one option to warn him."

"But she is right." Emuna said, "Our families, our loved ones, they are still there." she looked at Elah, tears stinging at her eyes once again, "We cannot just leave them. You would not leave them...right?"

Elah looked at Emuna, his own eyes glossy. "I would not leave them, but they would leave me."

Emuna bit back a sob as Elah's words crashed into her heart.

"They do not trust me, daughter, I cannot save those who refuse to be saved. Forcing against their will would go against my own law." Elah said, his voice filled with sorrow and regret. "Therefore, they will stay with the Anikulum."

Emuna could not bear looking into his eyes anymore for they were filled with more pain than even her own. The first of her sobs broke through the cave. Brian placed his hand on Emuna and she turned to him, crying into his kind embrace.

Elah watched silently, no words needed to be spoken. Tears of the ones lost ran down his own face. The streams of sadness trickled down his cheeks and glistened, even in the dark cave. He cried, for he knew their pain, Emuna's and those captured. Yet, to follow his own law, he could not end the agony. He did what was permitted by the law, now it was their choice.

"Get to Brian. If you control him, you control all of them." said a raspy, deep voice.

"Yes, sir." came the reply of a normal, human-sounding voice.

The room in which the two men spoke was too dark to see their faces, though the pure evil in the room was as clear as the light of day. The darkness was more than just darkness, it was a cover, it was keeping something hidden.

"You can swear on your life that you will be able to overpower Brian?" the evil voice said.

"Yes, sir, anybody can overpower that coward."

Brian walked through the forest, his feet making little noise against the leaves. He would pause every few steps and listen, waiting for any animal to come into hearing distance. He held Emuna's bow and arrow in his hands.

After talking with Elah for a few minutes he had decided to go hunting. Emuna was still distraught about her family and Brian felt helpless not being able to comfort her, his only defense was to get away for a bit.

As he tiptoed through the forest, many things crossed his mind. He couldn't keep his thoughts straight; a rabbit ran past him and he hardly noticed. Something was making him lose focus, but he did not know what.

A nearby chuckle made Brian pause in his walk, his hand tightened around the bow and arrow until his knuckles were white, and his hands began to glow a very light color. He stood still, his breathing shallow and silent.

"My boy, what a pleasure to see you again." the familiar voice of a man echoed through the forest and rang in Brian's ears.

Brian's heart stopped.

"I'd wondered where you'd been. You disappeared quite suddenly; I thought you being so cowardly had finally caught up to you." the man laughed, his voice now right behind Brian. "I was glad I did not have to teach you that lesson, but then I was disappointed to find out you were back. Such a disappointment you are, Brian."

Brian turned around, his hands now so bright that you could not see them. He saw a tall, brown-haired man with piercing eyes that borrowed themselves into his soul. The man stared down at him. He was taller than Brian and certainly more menacing. Brian stood still, frozen.

"Greetings, coward." the man said, showing a toothy grin. The man's hands curled into fists.

Brian stared up at the man. After what felt like an hour of silence, he finally found his voice, "Father, what is it that you want? I did not know you were safe."

"Well, I did not make it your business to know I was safe, but now you know." the man continued to taunt, "If you did not think I was safe, why did you not come after me, I wonder."

"There was no hope." Brian said, "Those captured were most likely dead, there was nothing I could have done had you been captured."

The man chuckled, "I doubt you cared, anyways. Just like you to forsake me, my useless son."

Brian sighed, "You abandoned me long ago. Why would I try to save you? Do I have any reason? Is there any memory I have forgotten that might give me motive to risking my life for you-"

Brian's sentence was cut off when the man gave him a

strong punch. Brian stepped back a half a step, his nose starting to bleed and his vision threatening to fog. The light in his hands vanished as he lost his sense of concentration.

"I am your father; you are my son; you are to save me no matter what you may think of me. And you are never to run your mouth in front of me," the man said, his voice was deep and furious. "Is that clear?"

Brian caught his breath and looked up at the man, a small spark of anger in his eyes. "Yes, sir." he said through clenched teeth.

"Good man." the man said, his voice was now light and almost sounded friendly. "Now, take me to your friends. I get bored of wandering these woods alone. Lead me forth."

Brian hesitated.

"Are you deaf?" the man said, "I command you, take me to your friends! Or must I give you more than just a small punch?" he lifted his fist in warning.

Brian unconsciously flinched and took another half step back. He nodded courteously then turned around and headed back towards the caves, his hands once again glowing a menacing white.

CHAPTER FIFTEEN

A STAINED SWORD

When Brian was close enough to the cave to see the entrance but not be heard, he stopped. He wished he could turn around and quickly end the man that stood behind him, but he couldn't. He simply stood still.

"Why did you stop?" the man asked roughly.

Brian turned around, "Why did you come here?" He looked the man in the eyes. Those cold, heartless eyes that sent memories shooting through Brian like volts of electricity. He flinched, but stood his ground.

"Why do you think I came here?" the man said, his eyes staring into Brian's, never moving.

"You and I both know why you are here." Brian said as his hand tightened around the bow and arrow he held. "And I am not going to let you do it."

The man glared at Brian for a moment and Brian stared back.

Suddenly, the man shoved Brian aside and walked forward. "We cannot just stand here all day. Come on." he said in a deep monotone.

Brian blinked a few times to clear his mind then ran to catch up with the man. When they reached the cave opening, Brian's father did not hesitate to go inside, Brian was close on his heels.

When they walked in, Emuna was the first to look up. Her eyes told Brian everything before she even spoke. The simple look Brian had on his face had told Emuna something was wrong. Something, but she did not know what. She turned from Brian to study the man he had brought with him, suspicions filled her mind.

David stood up and walked toward Brian and his father. "Greetings." he said cheerfully, "Who might you be?"

As his father introduced himself, Brian looked around the room, resting his eyes on Elah. The friendly leader stood beside Emuna, his eyes seeming to watch everything. While Brian had expected to see friendliness in his eyes, he did not. He saw something else, something he hadn't seen before. The look can only be described as the look of a victim awaiting retribution to be done on his tormentor. Sadness, anger, and justice.

Emuna's voice caught Brian's attention, "So you are Brian's father?" she said timidly, walking up to the man that stood beside Brian.

"Yes." the man said, drawing out the word.

Emuna smiled, "Pleasure to meet you." she curtsied slightly, though her wounds prevented her from doing a full curtsy, "I have heard much about you."

"Is that so?" the man said, "I am afraid I know little of you. We must mend this sometime-"

Brian cut-off the rest of the sentence, "Emuna, how

are you feeling?" he asked, walking over to her and subconsciously beginning to check the cuts on her arms.

"Better." she said.

"Well, Sir Aaron." David said to Brian's father, "Do you care to come with me to find some food since it appears that Master Brian's hunting trip has been a fruitless one?"

After Aaron and David came back with a few birds to eat, everybody settled down for dinner. Brian did not eat anything, though David attempted to persuade him. He claimed he had an upset stomach, and managed to avoid eating. Emuna talked with Aaron a lot, though she stayed close to Brian, a smile set on her face. Maeve and David talked some, but were soon tired and both went to bed. And Elah watched, silently.

After Elah having not spoken a word since Aaron's arrival hours before, Brian began to wonder if his father had even noticed Elah. Then he began to wonder if not noticing Elah would be a bad thing.

"I think I shall go for a walk." Elah suddenly said, the sound of his voice silencing the cave. He did not sound, as he always did, with a sweet, melodic tune, but, rather, his voice sounded deep and like a warning as if he knew something was to happen. "I will be back in a few hours. Brian shall be the head while I am gone, unless David wakes."

Before anybody could respond - or had the nerves to respond - Elah stood up and left the cave. His shadow vanished into the woods.

The cave stood silent for a few moments afterwards, nobody sure what to say, if anything. It was Aaron who finally broke the pause.

"So, Emuna." he began, holding each word as if he were trying to emphasize something. Brian tensed. "What is it that Brian has told you about me?"

Emuna's smile faded quickly and she completely gave up on the act she had been putting on. "What do you think he has told me?"

Aaron sighed and stood up, towering over Emuna, "I was afraid of that."

"Afraid of what? At least he had the chance to tell someone!" Emuna scolded, standing up, though the man still stood taller than her. "You hurt him and not just with punches and daggers! You rejected him!" she continued to yell, hardly realizing the cold look that crossed over Aaron's face and the dagger that he slid out of his belt. "How could you do that? To your own son no less!"

Before Emuna could continue, a strong slap from the man caused her to fall, her wounds sending a shockwave of pain through her. Tears threatened to fall from her eyes as she looked up at the man, glaring at him with all of her defiance.

Brian watched, unsure of his every breath. His fingers curled around the hilt of his sword as he looked from Emuna to his father. He saw no way to stop him. No way, at least, that he wanted to go.

Aaron reached down and grabbed Emuna off the ground, she struggled against him and tried to fight him, but he merely chuckled at her silly antics. Before she could fight back, he pushed her against the cave wall. She bit her lip, trying not to cry out from the wounds that stung her with every movement.

Aaron placed a dagger against Emuna's throat faster than she could catch her breath. He growled at her, his angry eyes piercing into hers. "Brian deserved every blow I gave him. He turned down his own family for books."

Emuna shuddered as the dagger was pressed deeper into her.

"You, on the other hand, deserve to die for speaking to me in such a manner. And you will." Aaron pressed the dagger tighter against Emuna's neck, having every intention to slit her throat in the slowest way possible.

Brian watched the blood begin to trickle from under her chin and he tightened his grip on his sword hilt. Everything told him that killing was wrong, but something stronger - and deep inside him - told him that there was no choice. Something else told him that protection came before comfort.

"Brian!" Emuna called, her voice strained and high from the pain that scorched through her body. She gasped for breath and only managed to make the dagger cut deeper into her neck.

Brian stopped thinking and his own debates and worries were pushed aside before he realized what he was doing. He drew his sword and quickly swung it towards his father's neck, the sharp blade glistening in the moonlight. It made contact with its victim and was stained with crimson blood. Removing head from body.

Brian let Emuna sit near the fire as he attempted to clean up the mess he had made, David and Maeve still asleep. He managed to take his father's body out of the cave, Emuna averting her eyes from the sight the entire time.

After he was done cleaning everything up as best he could, Brian sat down next to Emuna. His hands were stained with red liquid and his clothes bore the mark of blood as well. He sighed wearily as the two of them sat in silence, neither knowing what to say.

Emuna looked up when she heard gentle footsteps behind her.

Elah walked into the cave, not seeming surprised at the blood stains on the floor. He looked at Emuna and smiled at her.

Sheepishly, she smiled back, glancing at Brian to see if he would say anything.

He sat still, staring at the ground intently, as if his whole world depended on the small piece of cave floor he was studying.

Emuna sighed and looked up at Elah, silently asking him what to do.

Elah walked over to Brian, "You did what was right." he told him, his voice solemn yet comforting.

"I murdered." Brian stated coldly, not looking up at Elah.

"Your father chose death when he threatened you. One cannot change what is chosen by another." Elah said, "You did what was necessary."

Brian sighed, "I did what my impulses told me to."

Elah sat down beside Brian, causing Brian to look up at him. "You protected those close to you and yourself. Your father was a murderer and unrepentant. His punishment was death. You cannot change that, as you could not when you drew your sword."

CHAPTER SIXTEEN

SHATTERED HEART PIECES

Gavin argued with Taranis as they walked through the last of the mountain's foothills.

"I do not see a good reason why I cannot ride you!" Gavin complained.

Taranis kept his eyes straight ahead, not looking down at the little human that walked by his feet, annoying him till he prayed to Elah that he would suddenly go deaf and not have to hear Gavin's endless torments. "Because we are on an uncertified mission, following a person I do not believe is who he said he is, on our way to the castle of the most evil force in all of Chevl'Set. That, Gavin, is why you cannot ride me. I go with you only for protection, not as a pet pony."

Gavin groaned loudly. "You are intolerable!"

The dragon looked offended and glanced at Gavin. "I am intolerable, am I? Need I remind who has been complaining - without pause - for a full day now?"

"I would complain less if you let me ride you." Gavin grumbled.

"Aye, but you would not stop complaining entirely." Taranis said.

Gavin opened his mouth to protest when Taranis suddenly stopped walking and sat still, watching for something. He took deep breaths and scanned the sky and ground with his big, blue eyes. His tail unconsciously swished back and forth, creating a small wind-like sound.

Gavin watched as well, falling silent if only for a moment.

They stood at the edge of a large plain, the flat ground stretched for miles. Not a tree nor animal was in sight. The only thing for miles was grass, green and fresh.

"What is it?" Gavin asked, his voice a low whisper.

"It is not what it is. It is what it is not." Taranis bent his head down so he could look Gavin in the eyes, "This is your final chance to turn around, Gavin. Once we pass this plain we shall rely on only each other and the strengths Elah has given us. Even I am of little power when we reach the dark and forbidden lands."

Gavin thought for a moment. Forcing down a gulp of saliva, he finally replied. "Can I ride you?"

Taranis chuckled, "No, and now I have an excuse worthy of your small intellect. Beyond these plains being high in the sky will get us caught; we do not want to alert Pavix of our presence sooner than we wish. Therefore, I shall not be flying from here on, unless it is necessary. This shall make it about a two weeks travel to reach the other side of this plain."

Gavin sighed, "Very well, then we go forth. Flying or no flying."

Taranis nodded and the two of them walked forward,

118

leaving the last of the safe lands behind and going into the deep and dark villainous plains. To the places Pavix ruled and evil hid. The forbidden territories.

When Maeve awoke, everything seemed to have a very prominent, tense essence. The simple feel of the cave was solemn. She was reminded of the day the Anikulum came and the hair on her neck stood up with fear.

As she sat up on the ground, she took in the sight. Brian stood next to Elah, his shirt stained with a red liquid. Elah spoke with David, both of them speaking in whispered but serious tones. Emuna sat on a boulder a little ways from the men, watching timidly, never offering her advice or opinion.

Maeve guessed that Emuna would probably be the best one to talk to right now, so she walked over to the young girl and sat down beside her.

Emuna looked at Maeve and the elder could now see the tears in the young girl's eyes. Maeve's heart ached for the girl as she pieced together what had happened during her slumber. "Oh, sweetheart, I am sorry you had to see such a frightful thing." Maeve said.

Emuna didn't respond, but looked back at the ground, her body shivering with a held back sob.

Maeve was about to speak, but never let a word out as Elah's voice filled her ears.

"Maeve, good morning." Elah said, his voice calm, but Maeve could still hear the strained tone in it. "I trust you slept well."

Maeve nodded.

Elah smiled, "Very well..." he said, "Then come, all of you. You must not wait any longer to leave on your journey, lest Gavin entangle himself in more evil than is possible to be defeated."

Maeve stood up as Brian helped Emuna up. She caught a glimpse of the cut on Emuna's neck.

Elah led the three out of the cave and into the forest. The day was bright and the sun shone through the tree canopy. For the first time since the Anikulum had arrived, Maeve heard the songs of birds and the trampling of deer feet as they walked through the woods. It was once again a peaceful and calm world, one that settled softly in Maeve's heart and put her at ease, as well as the rest of the group.

They walked beside a river for some time before reaching a beach. Palm trees lined the sand and swayed in the wind. The waves crashed against some rocks on the shoreline and salty, beach air breezed over the travelers.

Elah did not stop where the waves met the shore, but he kept walking into the water, David close behind him. Emuna, Brian, and Maeve hesitated before going in too, a few feet behind the others.

Elah stopped when the water was about waist height, wetting the edges of Emuna's hair. Everybody looked quizzically at each other, unsure what the powerful man was doing.

Within a few moments, the water began to grow more choppy. Soon the white tips of waves were reaching them, though the travelers were past the wave break. They all watched intently as a shadowy figure of a large animal began to grow closer.

Emuna and Brian's breath stopped and Maeve felt her heart go to her throat as the head of what appeared to be a dragon slowly rose from the sea. Soon, the dragon's wings came out of the water, and the long, snake-like neck was entirely visible.

The creature that stood before them was, indeed, a form of dragon. It had light green eyes that reflected the water. Its wings appeared to be made of a soft, velvet-like material and it fluttered them gently as it studied the humans before it. When the animal breathed out, steam came from its nostrils and its scaly skin was tinted a deep blue that camouflaged with the water quite well.

The animal bowed its head to Elah and spoke with a soft voice, "Hello, my Master." came the feminine voice of the animal.

Elah nodded courteously and motioned towards the ones behind him.

The dragon looked at the others and smiled, "Greetings; my name is Avneet. It is a pleasure to meet all of you."

Elah turned around so his back was facing the dragon as he spoke. "Avneet is a Taninim dragon, one of the many hidden, dragon races in your lands." he said, "It is now time for her to come from hiding. No being has ever seen a Taninim, you shall be the first of the knowledgeable races, well learned in Chevl'Set's history and wise in my laws..."

As Elah spoke Emuna carefully studied Avneet. The dragon

tilted her head and looked at Emuna as the human watched her.

To Emuna, Avneet seemed dangerous, yet, somehow, she also seemed friendly, not as harsh or violent as Taranis had seemed, but perhaps it was because Avneet could speak. Within a few moments, Emuna began to wonder if Taranis could speak and soon Elah's words were no more than slurred sentences she did not pay attention to.

Emuna woke from her thoughts when Avneet stirred and the water began to move again. Elah was just finishing speaking.

"Avneet shall fly you to the plains past Shamayim, then you all must walk, but she shall stay with you for protection. If you go fast enough, you may be able to reach Gavin before..."

Elah's voice slowly faded, when clouds suddenly covered the sun. The water began to move franticly, as if a storm was approaching, and rain pelted the surface of the ocean, causing everyone to be wet from head to toe.

Lightning flashed and thunder rumbled in a threatening response. Avneet seemed to suddenly grow uneasy and Elah's face turned solemn.

Emuna turned to look behind her when the sound of clanking metal reached her ears. She felt her face lose all color and her legs seemed as if they would give out from underneath her as she looked at the sight before her.

There, on the shore, stood an army of thousands of Anikulum, all of them moving as one, large, black armed force. Hundreds of thousands white and heartless eyes stared at them, threatening war; promising death.

This was the second time Emuna had seen the eyes of an Anikulum and her body shuddered at the memory of her brother. She felt a tear crease down her cheek and plop into the water silently.

Elah's voice was slow and calming, "I cannot fight for you this time. I will always be with you and I will leave you my strength, but it is your choice as to what you do with it. Be wise."

Everybody tore their eyes from the Anikulum army just in time to see Elah vanish in a small flash of light, leaving no more than water at the place he had stood. They held their breaths in wonder, forgetting the army for a moment, until Avneet spoke.

"We must go, but I cannot carry all of you." she said hurriedly, "I must leave two behind for I can only hold two."

"You cannot call for another dragon?" Brian asked.

Avneet shook her head, "They will not come out of hiding for me. The Taninim dragons only listen to Elah."

"Then why didn't he leave us another dragon?" Emuna said, panic clear in her voice, "He should have called another one!"

"Stay calm, m'dear." Avneet said, "He knew what he was doing; his plans never falter."

An arrow with a bright red feather flew above the water, shot by one of the Anikulum's archers. It was barely visible as it glided along at a shockingly fast speed. It rushed through the air in a matter of seconds though the seconds seemed like hours.

Emuna watched silently, hearing the whistling of the arrow as it flew towards the small group and towards David.

The arrow hit David in the back and buried itself deep

into him, causing him to take in a small gasp from the pain that was sent through him. Soon, blood trickled from his wound and slipped into the water, tainting the clear ocean a light shade of pink and turning his white shirt red.

David took a breath, attempting to gather himself, but only managed to grimace at the action.

"David?" Emuna asked, starting to walk towards him, but she was stopped by Brian.

"You two...should go." David finally said, his voice raspy and tight with pain, "Gavin needs your help... I have...served my purpose...but you... have much more before you."

Emuna looked at Brian pleadingly, waiting for him to say something.

Brian glanced at Emuna then looked back to David, "Yes, Sir. We will go, but what of Lady Maeve?"

Maeve spoke up before David could, "I will stay here with him." she said, "Such a great soldier does not deserve to die alone. You must go. Go with Avneet and find Gavin; I will stay with David."

David would have protested had not he been so weak, instead, all he managed was a faint smile.

Emuna took in a deep breath and walked over to David. She gave him a gentle hug, "Thank you for everything."

David could not rush Emuna onward and the only response he managed was a small whisper, the words heard only by Emuna, "Never stop searching."

Emuna nodded slightly and let go of David, backing away and standing towards Brian.

Before Brian and Emuna decided to stay as well, Avneet carefully picked both of them up with her mouth and put them on her back. Emuna clung tightly to the dragon, afraid of falling when she took off.

Avneet made a gentle purring sound in the direction of Maeve and David before spreading her wings and gently lifting off the ground. She rose off the ocean floor with all the majestic beauty of an eagle, leaving behind all that was dear to her two riders.

The original flight was not, as Emuna had expected, rough. Avneet was very careful to fly gently so as not to scare her riders and Emuna was glad of this.

They had not been flying for more than five minutes before the Anikulum army vanished behind them, along with the shore and their friends. Emuna hung her head solemnly and let tears stream down her face as two more lives were taken by the Anikulum and another piece of her heart was shattered.

CHAPTER SEVENTEEN

NEW CHALLENGES AWAIT

Gavin dragged his feet as he walked behind Taranis, groaning and complaining with every step. "We have been walking for days." he moaned, "How long will it take to cross this plain?"

Taranis sighed, "I already told you..."

Gavin whined some more, "Fine, but how long do we have *left*?"

Taranis stopped and turned to face Gavin, "The same amount of time we had left two hours ago when you asked me, five more days, but if you keep dragging your feet as you are then we will never reach the end of this plain. Come." He pushed Gavin with his paw, softly, but strong enough to cause Gavin to stumble.

Gavin glared at Taranis, "I am trying my hardest!" he protested.

Taranis shook his head, "No, you are not, but that is fine. I will now walk at a normal speed. You can stay here if you wish...and get eaten by Lupi." Taranis turned and began to stroll away.

Gavin watched him, wide-eyed, for a moment before

running to catch up with him, "Fine, fine, fine." he said, "I will walk faster."

Taranis smiled, but did not turn to look at Gavin, "Good human."

Maeve carefully led David to a few rocks that sat in the middle of the ocean. She sat down on the rocks, letting David rest his head on her lap as his breathing slowed.

The Anikulum army still stood at the shoreline, but they had now begun to beat drums together, the deep tone of the instrument causing the water to shake and quiver. The rain ceased, but the sun remained covered by clouds and the birds' songs had stopped.

Maeve brushed away the hair from David's forehead as he groaned with pain, his face contorted in a grimace. "David?" Maeve whispered, attempting to grasp his attention, "It helps if you speak. With the pain, I mean. If you think of something else."

David smiled and opened his eyes just for a moment to see Maeve, "What is it you wish me to...speak of?" he managed to ask softly.

Maeve thought for a moment, "Tell me of your past. What of your family?"

David sighed and let out a small moan when the simple action of breathing hurt him, "My parents have long passed... My father at the age of one hundred and thirty four and my mother at the...young age of one hundred and ten."

"Young? That age is old in the human village." Maeve said.
The beating of the Anikulum drums grew louder as the two spoke and, slowly, each Anikulum drew their sword.

"Do you...know your...age?" David asked, grimacing and shutting his eyes tighter.

Maeve chuckled, "Mm...no, I do not. I have forgotten my own past. Some say it was taken from me. Though, I wish to know more of you. Do you have a wife?"

David opened his eyes and looked at Maeve for a moment, "Why do you ask...Lady Maeve?" he said, unable to keep his eyes open, he closed them again.

"Because when one is facing a challenge, thinking of the one you love can give you the strength to make it through said challenge." Maeve said.

David coughed and turned his head away from Maeve, "I... am...married...but my wife...is...she was taken, long, long ago."

"Oh..." Maeve said, "What did she look like?"

"Blonde hair..." David whispered, speaking was growing impossible, "Green eyes... Kind and wise... Like... You." David's hand began to slip from his stomach.

Maeve's eyes widened at David's words and the memories of a hundred years played before her. She gasped. "David..." she said.

Maeve looked down at David. His eyes were closed and his chest did not move with the intake or release of breath as his hand slipped from his stomach and landed in the water. A thin smile was set on his lifeless face

Avneet flew for a day, waiting until the sun went down to stop and rest for the night. She landed softly on the ground and crouched down to let Brian and Emuna slip off her back.

Brian jumped off Avneet then helped Emuna down. Avneet stood up fully and stretched as Brian and Emuna busied themselves making a fire.

After a fire was set up and Brian and Emuna were comfortably settled down beside Avneet for warmth, Emuna spoke for the first time since they'd left Realta.

"Should we be stopping at night, Avneet? What of the Lupi?" she asked.

Avneet curled up and rested her head on the ground, closing her eyes calmly as she spoke. "The Lupi are not dumb animals, they would not dare attack a Taninim. We are peace-loving dragons, but are, nevertheless, not safe to be around when angered. I will protect you to the death, m'dear."

Emuna sighed contently and leaned her head on Avneet's stomach, hearing the dragon's slow heartbeat against her ear. "May I ask you a final question?"

"Of course." Avneet said.

"How long do you suppose it will take us to reach Gavin?"

Avneet sighed, "Two weeks at most. Now, you should rest." Avneet turned around and gently nudged Emuna with her nose before covering her with her wing. "You have a long life ahead of you."

Emuna closed her eyes and quickly fell into a deep sleep.

Brian had listened to the conversation, but still decided that he would still stay awake and be on watch until he too fell asleep.

So dragon and Lumenian slept on the ground that night, resting for the long days ahead of them and the many more wars they would fight before Elah's great plan was complete. Before they were free from the invisible bindings that held them to the imperfections of Chevl'Set and submitted them to the temptations of Pavix.

Made in the USA
Charleston, SC
23 January 2012